D1617418

The Portrait

Joan Wolf

Untreed
Reads

The Portrait
By Joan Wolf

Copyright 2020 by Joan Wolf
Cover Copyright 2020 by Untreed Reads Publishing
Cover Design by Ginny Glass

ISBN-13: 978-1-94913-526-8

Published by Untreed Reads, LLC
506 Kansas Street, San Francisco, CA 94107
www.untreedreads.com

Also available in ebook.

Printed in the United States of America.

Without limiting the rights under copyright reserved above, no part of this publication may be reproduced, stored in or introduced into a retrieval system, or transmitted, in any form, or by any means (electronic, mechanical, photocopying, recording, or otherwise), without the prior written permission of both the copyright owner and the above publisher of this book.

If you purchased this book without a cover, you should be aware that this book is stolen property. It was reported as "unsold and destroyed" to the publisher and neither the author nor the publisher has received any payment for the "stripped book."

The scanning, uploading, and distribution of this book via the Internet or via any other means without the permission of the publisher is illegal and punishable by law. Please purchase only authorized electronic editions, and do not participate in or encourage electronic piracy of copyrighted materials. Your support of the author's rights is appreciated.

Publisher's Note

This is a work of fiction. Names, characters, places, and incidents either are the product of the author's imagination or are used fictitiously, and any resemblance to actual persons, living or dead, business establishments, events, or locales is entirely coincidental.

The publisher does not have any control over and does not assume any responsibility for author or third-party websites or their content.

Also by Joan Wolf and Untreed Reads Publishing

The American Earl

The Reluctant Earl

The Master of Grex

The Heiress

A London Season

His Lordship's Mistress

The Guardian

The Pretenders

Golden Girl

www.untreedreads.com

Note on Classical Equitation

Today we call Isabel's style of riding *dressage*. It is very beautiful and has been practiced in Europe for centuries. Basically, it is the classical art of riding. To quote one of the greatest riders and trainers of all time, Alois Podhajsky: "The object of the classical art of riding is to train a horse not only to be brilliant in the movements and exercises of the High School, but also to be quiet, supple, and obedient." (*Complete Training of Horse and Rider in the Principles of Classical Horsemanship*, Wilshire Book Company, 1967, 1982.) The Spanish Riding School in Vienna is the most well-known of all the European schools today.

This is the kind of riding Isabel espouses. Alonzo is at what we would today call "Grand Prix" level. Dressage today is one of the equestrian Olympic sports. An interesting fact: the equestrian sports are the only Olympic sport where men and women directly compete against each other. It's all about the horse.

If you would like to see what Grand Prix dressage looks like, go to YouTube and type in *Charlotte Dujardin's World Breaking Freestyle Test at London's Olympia*. She and her great horse Valegro are the pair who were my model for Isabel and Alonzo. Every time I watch that video I get chills up and down my spine—it is that amazing.

Prologue

Isabel stood next to her horse, the reins held firmly in her hand. "Don't be nervous," her father said to her in the French language that was their native tongue. "This is just another ride with Alonzo. You've done it a hundred times. Pretend this is just another performance in Le Cirque Equestre and you'll be fine."

The big white horse Isabel was holding nodded his head as if in agreement with Pierre Besson, owner of the circus. Isabel and Alonzo had worked together for three years and the rumors of their excellence had reached Britain. Their reputation, and that of the entire Cirque Equestre, had been so impressive that Astley's Royal Amphitheatre in London, the premiere horse circus in the world, had invited Pierre's company to perform at their arena. Tonight would be their first performance.

The Bessons had been impressed by Astley's spectacular show. A traveling circus such as the Cirque Equestre could never compete with what was staged in Astley's huge amphitheater. The number of riders, the number of horses, the costumes, the scenery…it would be impossible for a circus that traveled from town to town to equal such extravagance.

Isabel said, "Everything in this show has been so exciting, Papa. Perhaps the audience will find us boring."

"Nonsense," Pierre returned stoutly. "They will love you."

The props for the previous scene had been cleared away and it was Isabel's turn. She was the last act on the program and her ride had been advertised all over London. The orchestra, which was placed below a stunning arch that overlooked the ring, began to play her music. Alonzo heard it and his ears flicked back and forth.

It was time. Isabel allowed her father to give her a leg up into the saddle. As soon as she took up the reins she could feel Alonzo's anticipation. He was a magnificent gray Andalusian stallion, and he loved his job. She patted his muscular neck, took up a contact, and horse and rider made their entrance. The buzz of the crowd quieted as they turned their attention to the ring.

Pierre stood in the entryway and watched as his daughter advanced to the center of the large arena. Alonzo's trot was so incredibly light that he appeared almost weightless. Horse and rider came to a perfect halt, and Pierre sent up a prayer to the lord that this English audience would appreciate the beauty they were about to witness.

Isabel and Alonzo had a bond Pierre had never before seen between rider and horse. When she was on his back, it was as if they were one creature, not two. By the time Isabel had reached sixteen she had proved to be such a talented rider that one of the riding masters from Saumur, the French national riding school, had seen fit to teach her and Alonzo. This was something that had never happened before, and would probably never happen again. If she had been a boy, they would certainly have invited her into the school.

She was dressed today in fawn-colored breeches, a tailored black coat and high black riding boots. Her dark hair lay against the back of her coat in a long plait. Her white-gloved hands were slightly raised, and it seemed as if her body and leg position never changed. Pierre watched with swelling pride as girl and horse went through their program: from passage to extended trot, to piaffe, to half pass, to piaffe again, to canter to canter pirouette, back to half pass and then to canter changes of lead on every stride. The music that accompanied them enhanced every change in speed and gait.

Alonzo, a solidly built horse, seemed to float across the ground.

The amphitheater was silent. Even the children, and there were always children at Astley's, were quiet. When Isabel cantered to the center of the ring and halted, giving Alonzo a hearty pat on his neck, a great roar came from the crowd. A shiver of pride ran up and down Pierre's back as he watched his daughter take Alonzo around the perimeter of the floor, waving at the crowd as she passed by. Alonzo walked along with his neck stretched out in front of him, blowing contentedly through his nostrils. He had been brilliant, and he knew it.

Father and daughter retired to bed that evening with a mixture of exultation and relief. They were thrilled that the English audience had been able to appreciate Alonzo's excellence. Neither of them knew that Isabel's appearance at Astley's would have a much further reaching effect than either of them had ever dreamed.

Chapter One

Two weeks after my first performance at Astley's, a be-wigged footman garbed in magnificent blue and silver livery appeared at the door of the hotel room where Papa and I were staying. "Monsieur Besson?" the vision inquired, bowing.

"Oui," Papa said.

I got up from the sofa and went to stand behind Papa. What on earth could this footman want with us?

He handed Papa an envelope and bowed again. "From the Earl of Camden, Monsieur. I am to wait for a reply."

"What is it?" Papa asked.

"I have a message for you from the Earl of Camden," the footman repeated. "I will await your reply."

"Come in," said Papa, and he moved away from the door so the footman could enter. I stood close as he opened the folded page of the letter. There was an engraved crest on the top of the stationery page.

Papa folded the paper again and stared into space, saying nothing.

"Papa!" I couldn't contain my curiosity. "What does it say?"

"The Earl of Camden has invited us to his London house. He will send a carriage for us tomorrow at eleven o'clock."

I stared at my father. "Do you know the Earl of Camden, Papa?"

"No."

"Then why is he inviting us to his house?"

"I have no idea, Isabel."

There was a strained look on my father's face.

"Perhaps he saw Alonzo's performance and wants to ask about his training?"

Some of the strain left Papa's face. "That may be true. These English are such terrible riders. They sit on their horses' haunches and stick their legs out in front of them." He clicked his tongue and shook his head. "I don't know how their cavalry ever managed to keep their horses under control; the poor creatures must have been miserable with all that weight bearing down on their kidneys."

"They need a riding school like Saumur."

"They need to find instructors to teach at such a riding school."

We seemed to have got off the topic of the invitation. I said, "We should accept this invitation, Papa. An earl is a powerful man. We cannot afford to alienate such a person."

"You are right little one," he said with a sigh. "If you made an impression on such a man, it can only be good for us." And he gave the splendid footman our reply.

*

I don't have a wardrobe that embraces visits to the nobility, but I did the best I could. Elisabeth, the wonderful woman who had taken care of me since my mother died, helped me. We decided on a dark gold dress. It was old but still in good repair. May in England was colder than May in France, but I had a brown cloak that had belonged to my mother that looked all right.

"This invitation—it is very strange is it not?" Elisabeth asked as she brushed my hair.

"Very," I agreed. I told her about my idea that the earl might be interested in our training methods.

"I hope that is all he is interested in," Elisabeth said darkly.

"What do you mean?"

"I mean this earl may think you are a circus girl and want something other than horse training from you. It is a good thing your Papa is going with you."

"I didn't think of that," I said. I would have thought of it had I been invited by myself. You cannot travel with a circus and not be aware of what goes on between a man and a woman outside of marriage. But our circus was a close-knit group. There were riders and grooms we took on and let go, but the core of the circus had remained the same since I was small.

Finding a hat to match the dress and cloak was difficult. Then I remembered that Papa had a beret almost the same color as the cloak. I put it on, and Elisabeth thought it looked very well.

When I was ready, I looked into the mirror in my small bedroom. I was not fool enough to think I looked like a lady of fashion, but at least everything matched.

"Are you ready, Isabel?" my father called.

"Yes, Papa. I am coming."

He regarded me, head to one side, when I presented myself.

"It's the best we could do, Papa," I said apologetically.

"It is I who should apologize to you little one, for not buying you the clothes you deserve. But no matter what you are wearing, Isabel, you will always be beautiful."

He said this very gravely and I slipped my arm through his. "Come, Papa, let us find out what this earl wants."

*

The Earl of Camden's house was in Grosvenor Square. We drove there in a shiny black coach pulled by four lovely gray horses. I was curious about their breeding and thought I would ask the earl about them if I had an opportunity. I looked out the window as we drove through Mayfair, a part of London I had never seen. The houses were splendid, the streets were clean, and there were trees and well-kept gardens everywhere. Grosvenor Square, when we reached it, was impressive. A variety of houses were built around a very large garden. Some of the houses were magnificent and others more ordinary. The house we stopped in front of was one of the magnificent ones.

We descended to the curb, and walked toward the tall stone house. I was still wondering what in the world we were doing here, when Papa stopped me. The strained look was back on his face. "Whatever happens, Isabel, you must remember that your *Maman* and I loved you with all our hearts."

"I know, Papa," I said, a little bewildered by why he was saying such a thing here. "I love you with all my heart too."

The front door opened before we reached it and a tall, heavy man with white hair greeted us. "Monsieur, Mademoiselle, if you will please accompany me to the drawing room."

"Of course," Papa said in English.

Both Papa and I spoke English fairly well. One of our riders, who had been with us for years, was English. Papa had taught him to ride in the French way, and Charles had taught us English. I had also learned some German and Spanish from the circus people who came and went as the years passed.

I looked around as we proceeded through the house toward the drawing room. The foyer had black and white tiles on the floor and was very grand, as was the circular staircase that came after it. The butler stopped before the arched entrance to one of the rooms that opened off the hallway and announced, "Monsieur and Mademoiselle Besson, my lord."

I didn't notice the room, I was too focused on the man who had turned from the window and was coming toward us. He was tall and broad-shouldered with golden blond hair that caught the light from the window. He looked like a Greek god. *What on earth could a man like this want with us?*

He stopped in front of us, looked at me and said in French, "Thank you for coming."

He was looking at me, not Papa, so I replied in the same language. "We are dying of curiosity to know why you wanted to see us, my lord."

The eyes that were looking at me were as blue as the sky at midday. He said softly, "I asked you to come, Mademoiselle, because I want to show you a portrait."

A portrait? I hoped my face didn't show my astonishment. Why on earth would an earl ask Papa and me to visit him so he could show us a portrait? Next to me Papa's sharp intake of breath echoed my feeling.

"I hope that will be all right with you, Monsieur Besson," the earl said courteously.

"*Certainement,*" Papa replied.

The earl gestured to a pale green wall before which an easel was set up. "It is right here," he said. "If you would come with me?"

I followed him and Papa came behind me. The earl had stepped away, so I was alone when I looked at the painting.

It was a portrait of me.

The earl's soft voice said, "I had it brought from my home in Berkshire after I had seen your performance. It is a portrait of my great-grandmother, done by Sir Joshua Reynolds. It hangs over the fireplace at Camden Hall, my residence in Berkshire. I've looked at it since I was a boy, so you can imagine my astonishment when I saw you ride at Astley's, Mademoiselle."

I didn't answer; I just kept staring at the portrait. The woman in the picture was dark-haired, with wide-set gray eyes and a thin, curved nose. She wore no jewelry and her rust-colored gown had a deep décolletage, exposing a long graceful neck and flawless skin. She looked like a queen beholding her subjects. She looked as if she owned the world.

"As you see, Mademoiselle," the earl said in a quiet voice, "you have the same features, the same eyes, the same nose. You could be twins."

I turned to my Papa, who had come to stand next to me. "What does this mean, Papa?" I asked in bewilderment.

It was the earl who replied. "I believe I have the answer to that question, and so does Monsieur Besson." The earl looked at my father, lifted a golden eyebrow and said, "Shall we talk?"

"*Oui*," Papa said wearily. "I suppose we must."

Chapter Two

The earl took us into a room that was filled with books. Normally I would have been delighted and asked if I could look at them, but at the moment I was much too anxious. The earl invited us to sit before the fireplace, which was giving off a welcome heat. I was feeling chilled; my hands were icy.

We sat on a soft leather sofa and faced the earl, who was seated on a similar sofa on the other side of a low table. He fixed his blue eyes on me and said in his excellent French, "I want to tell you a story, Mademoiselle. It is about my Aunt Maria."

I sat upright on the edge of my cushion. I had a sickening feeling that I did not want to hear about his Aunt Maria.

He leaned a little toward me and said, "When Maria was young, she married the Earl of Manchester, a man who was a good deal older than she. She was his second wife. He had one son from his first marriage, and he wanted another from Maria. She was married to the earl for eight years before she finally had a child—a girl. The earl was displeased but Maria was ecstatic. She had been praying for a child for many years and she could hardly believe her good fortune when little Charlotte came along."

I was listening, not sure what all this meant, but scared to find out. When the earl paused, I glanced sideways at Papa. He was looking stricken, which made me afraid. I put my hand over his and held tight.

The earl was continuing, "One day, while Maria and her husband were in London, one of the nursery maids took little Charlotte for an outing in her pram. According to the maid, she only turned her back for a few seconds, and when she looked back at the pram, the baby was gone."

I stared at the earl, afraid to breathe, afraid to move, afraid I would break into little pieces. I didn't want to hear any more, but the earl was holding my eyes and I couldn't seem to look away.

"You were that baby, Isabel," he said. "And your mother has been mourning you for all the years you have been alive."

I felt as if he had punched me in the stomach. I couldn't breathe. I shook my head in denial, turned to my father and said in a breaking voice, "Papa?"

He was hunched up like an old man, and his face was pinched and white when he looked at me.

"Papa?" I said again piteously. "Is this true? Please tell me it isn't true!"

"This is what happened, little one." Papa's voice was low and sad. "The circus I was attached to had played the south coast of England for the summer and we were all at the dock ready to return to France. When your *Maman* and I were about to board, a woman came up to us with a baby in her arms. She wanted to sell it to us."

I closed my eyes tightly. Please, please, don't let him say it. Dear God, don't let him say it.

Papa continued, "Of course I said no and turned away. But your *Maman* had reached out for the child and was holding it against her breast." He threw a brief glance at the earl. "Like your aunt, my wife had longed in vain for a child. Now she had a baby in her arms, a baby that could be hers. I looked at her and knew I could not deny her this gift from God. So I paid the woman what she wanted and we brought Isabel home with us to France."

I was frozen. I didn't know what to think, what to do. I wasn't Isabel Besson. I was someone else, the child of some

English aristocrat. From out of nowhere I heard myself saying, "I don't like the name Charlotte."

"I would never ask you to change your name, Isabel." The earl's voice was quiet. "But I would like you to come home with me. Your mother is still alive, and she deserves to see you. By birth you are Lady Char...Isabel Lewins, and your father left a bequest in his will for a generous sum of money to go to you should you ever be found."

"I don't want any money!" I flared.

He ignored me and turned his blue gaze to my father. "I would like Isabel to meet her natural family. I realize you had no idea of who she might be when you...adopted...her, but you must see she was done a great wrong. My aunt was done a great wrong."

"I understand," my father said. He was white as chalk. "Of course we always believed she was the child of the woman who was looking to sell her. We thought she would be in much better circumstances with us than she would have been with her natural mother."

"Then you won't object if I take Isabel to live with her family for a time. Her original family."

"I don't see how I can object," my father said in that unfamiliar small sad voice.

"*Papa!*" I cried in protest. He couldn't want me to go off with this strange man! We were going back to France. The circus was engaged to perform in Paris. I was the main attraction. He couldn't leave me in England.

I said all of this to Papa, but he didn't look at me. He said to the earl, "Where is your home, my lord?"

"Camden Hall in Berkshire. I live there with my brother Robert, Robert's wife and their two children, my Aunt

Augusta and my cousin Roger. Of course, I will invite my Aunt Maria for a visit so she can be reunited with her daughter."

"I am not going anywhere with you," I said loudly. "I don't care a fig about my birth. Papa has been my father for all of my life. I am not leaving him!"

"You must, little one," my father said. "Think of that poor woman, your mother, who has loved you and mourned for you for nineteen years while your *Maman* and I had the great joy of your presence." Papa turned back to the earl. "I do not regret a moment of those years, my lord. If we had not adopted Isabel, God knows whom that evil woman would have sold her to. But I think you are right. I think she needs to know the family of her birth."

"Papa! Think! In a month the circus is to perform in Paris. How will you fare without Alonzo's performance?"

"We will improvise."

I had a terrible thought. "Alonzo! You can't put another rider on Alonzo!"

"*Non*. Alonzo would not be Alonzo without you, Isabel." Papa took my hand and held it. "You can take Alonzo with you to this house where the earl lives. It will be good for the both of you to have a little rest from performing. I do not want him to become stale."

My eyes flew to the earl. "How long a stay are you proposing?"

"I think half a year would be fair. After all, as Monsieur just said, he has had you for nineteen years."

*

Papa and I went back to our hotel and argued. He wanted me to go, and I didn't understand why. After going around and around for what seemed like hours, Papa saying it would be a good thing for me, me saying it wouldn't, he said in that voice with which he kept all of his workers focused on their jobs: "Isabel, you must go. You are the daughter of an earl. You have been left some money. You now have the opportunity to live the life you were born for, the life that thieving servant girl stole from you. I believed I was doing a good thing when I took you from her, but now that I know the truth, I feel I have stolen from you as well."

I stared at him and for the first time noticed how tired he looked. I saw how many wrinkles there were in his beloved face. He had been thirty-seven when I was born. He was fifty-six now, and he had worked hard all his life. He was tired.

I said abruptly, "Papa, do you ever think of quitting the circus and retiring?"

His return smile was crooked. "Where did that come from?"

"I was just wondering."

He shook his head. "The circus is our income, Isabel. I cannot afford to give it up."

I remembered how relieved he had looked when Astley's wanted me for their show. They had paid quite a lot of money. I had never thought much about money, and Papa had never talked about money with me. We always seemed to have enough. But if he disbanded the circus, where would our money come from? Was he going to have to work hard for the rest of his life?

If there had been money left to me, I could use it to help Papa retire. Suddenly the visit to the earl's home took on a different light.

Papa had taken my hand into his warm one. "I have made inquiries about the earl," he said in a reassuring voice. "If I had heard he was a libertine, I would never allow this. But I have heard that he is a good man. little one. His reputation is unblemished. I will send Elisabeth with you so you won't feel lonesome; she will be a piece of home."

I bit my lip and nodded.

He leaned toward me. "You owe it to this family who was robbed of you to be kind. Do your best to make these six months a pleasant visit for both you and your new family and I will come and take you home after six months have passed."

I held onto his hand as if it was a lifeline. I blinked back tears and nodded. "I will show this family that I was brought up with the right values," I said in a wobbly voice. "I will make you proud, Papa."

His eyes glistened with tears as he took me into his arms. "You always make me proud, Isabel. You always make me proud."

Chapter Three

The earl wanted to leave London before word got out about my identity. "There will be a huge clamor," he said. "The newspapers will seize on it. Everyone who has seen you ride at Astley's will suddenly find they noticed your resemblance to my family. The thing to do is get you home to Camden Hall where you can be protected from any vulgar curiosity."

Camden Hall would never be my home, but I agreed with the rest of his idea. The sooner these six months was over the better. I would do my best to be pleasant to these people, but this visit wasn't going to change me. I would never be Lady Isabel. I was Isabel Besson now, and I would always be Isabel Besson. And my mother would always be *Maman*, who had loved me and who had left me too soon.

I was thinking this as I stood with the earl in the stable behind his London house. We had just moved Alonzo from the amphitheater stables to Grosvenor Square's. Alonzo had traveled through the busy London streets with equanimity. To a horse used to the sound of canons and fireworks—an occasional accompaniment to Papa's circus as well as Astley's—a walk through the busy London streets was not frightening; it was interesting. He had always been a curious horse, and I mentioned this to the earl as he closed the stall door behind Alonzo's muscled hindquarters.

"There are only a few things he objects to seriously," I said. "It's important for your stable people to know he hates cats."

We were leaning against Alonzo's stall door watching him eat hay. *"Cats?"* The earl turned to look at me. I am not short, but my head barely reached his chin. He had to be several inches over six feet. He lifted one golden eyebrow. "Why cats?"

I shrugged. "His aversion was firmly fixed by the time I got him as a three-year-old. It's a nuisance because stables need cats to keep down the rodents."

"I was thinking the same thing," the earl said. "How do you handle it?"

"We got a terrier to live in the stable. Her name is Penny and Alonzo adores her. She keeps the rats away."

"And where is Penny?"

"She just had a litter, so we left her in France." I tilted my chin to look at up him. "He misses her. Do you think we might get him another terrier?"

"Of course. If there is anything else you want—anything at all—just tell me and I'll arrange it."

What I wanted was something even this great earl couldn't arrange. I wanted my *Maman* and Papa to be my real parents. I wanted to be performing with Alonzo before a huge crowd of people, reducing them to silence by the incredible beauty of my horse. I wanted the life I had always led.

"Isabel." His voice was gentle. He had this way of saying my name that was different from anyone else's. I thought it might be in the way he pronounced *bel*. His voice seemed to linger on the syllable. "I know this is hard for you," he said. "You have led a wonderful life with two parents who loved you very much. You have had the opportunity to work with this amazing horse. Unfortunately, the same cannot be said for the mother who lost you. I told you a little about her when we first met. Her life has not been a happy one. Her first husband, the Earl of Mansfield, was a hard man. He had one son by his first wife, and he married Maria, who was much younger than he, so he could have more sons to ensure his heritage. Maria's only child was a girl—you. Mansfield blamed her for not giving him another son, then he blamed her for entrusting you to a careless nursemaid. His death was a happy release for her.

I wanted to ask him about the inheritance, but I thought it was too soon. Instead I said, "You said she married again?"

"Yes, to a Scot who lives in the Border country between England and Scotland. He's only a baronet and he doesn't have much money, but he seems to be a decent sort and Maria loves him. I didn't object to the match when she asked."

I looked at him in bewilderment. "Why on earth would you object to the match? You sound as if you're sorry that Maria had such a miserable first marriage. I should think you'd be happy she finally found happiness."

He gave me a puzzled look. "I *was* happy for her. That's why I agreed to it."

I nodded slowly, trying to figure out how this family worked. "Why did you let her marry the earl if he was such a *batard*?" I asked.

The earl gave me an amused look. "You will have to watch your vocabulary when you are at Camden, Isabel. Young ladies in England don't use words like bastard."

I shrugged.

He said, "I had nothing to do with Maria's first marriage. Her father, our grandfather, arranged that. He chose Mansfield because he was rich and owned large amounts of property. Those were the things that mattered to my grandfather."

"More than his daughter's happiness?"

"Yes." He looked down at me and smiled. "Look what you escaped when you were kidnapped. If you hadn't been, you might be married to a marquis by now. Or a duke."

I made a noise of dismissal. "A title is nothing to me." Alonzo turned his head to look at me. He was still chewing on his hay. I said in the voice I used only to him, "I'll bet that tastes good, big boy."

He threw his head up and down then turned back to the hay that was piled in the corner of his stall.

I said to the earl, "I don't want to be called 'Lady Isabel.' It makes me uncomfortable. It makes me feel like an imposter."

He said, "You're the daughter and sister of an earl. You'll get used to it."

The sister of an earl? I had a brother?

The earl was going on, "I have written to my aunt to advise her of your existence. I have also invited her to make a visit to Camden Hall so she can meet you."

My stomach and my throat tightened. I had known I would have to meet this foreign mother. The earl's announcement shouldn't have come as such a shock. But it did.

I swallowed, dipped my head in a brief nod, and silence fell. Alonzo ate his hay. At last I said, "If she lives in Scotland, why am I staying with you?"

"Because I am the head of Maria's family and it is proper for you to be under my roof. Your mother may stay with me for as long as she likes. It is her old home, after all."

I opened the stall door and slipped in to stand beside Alonzo. He looked up from his hay, acknowledged me with a flick of his ears, and went back to eating. He was accustomed to being in strange stalls, and as long as he knew I was nearby, he would be fine. I laid my hand on his neck, felt his warmth, his familiar smell, and wanted to bury my head in his mane and cry.

Instead I bent and picked up a few stalks of hay. "No wonder you're gobbling it up," I said, sniffing it. "It's gorgeous."

"When we get to the hall you will have to speak with Stoddard so he knows what to feed Alonzo," the earl said from the other side of the stall door.

"I most certainly will."

The earl had told me that Stoddard was the name of his Head Groom, the person in charge of the stables at Camden Hall. I planned to have a long, detailed chat with the man as soon as we arrived. Alonzo was a fairly adaptable horse—he was an Andalusian and the breed was known for its good temperament—but he was accustomed to me looking after him. I was going to have to make it clear what the earl's staff could do and what I was going to do myself.

I turned to horse-talk to keep the earl from speaking about family any more. "Alonzo needs to be turned out by himself and you cannot stable him next to a mare."

"I know," the earl replied with obvious patience. "You have told me this a dozen times already, Isabel. If you can't give me credit for knowing how to take care of a stallion at least give some credit to my staff."

I didn't trust him. I didn't trust his staff. The Cirque Equestre had performed at a few chateaux in France, so I knew the house was going to be at a distance from the stable. I wouldn't be able to run in and out to check on Alonzo as I was accustomed to. I wouldn't be able to take a nap curled up in the corner of his stall.

"Maybe I should leave him with Papa," I said in an anguished voice. "I'm being selfish wanting to keep him with me."

"Nonsense," the earl said.

His tone was crisp and dictatorial. I swung around to stare at him.

"Use your brain, Isabel," he said. "You need to ride Alonzo. If he is not ridden properly he will lose the muscle you have so painstakingly built up. There is no one else who is capable of keeping him in decent condition. He needs to be with you."

I didn't like his tone, but he was right. I was being an idiot. I glared at him to show what I thought of his manner, then turned and kissed Alonzo's neck. "I'll see you in the morning, big boy," I said.

Alonzo continued to munch on hay, and I returned to the earl's side. He looked down at me, amusement in his intensely blue eyes. "I'll drive you back to your hotel," he said.

I was to spend this last night in London with Papa. Tomorrow the earl would drive Elisabeth and me to his home in Berkshire, where I would be imprisoned for six months with a host of people I didn't know and didn't want to know.

And I had promised Papa to be kind to them.

Please God, I prayed, let me return home with enough money for Papa to retire.

Chapter Four

The earl's coach collected Elisabeth and me from the hotel the following morning at six o'clock. If all went well, the earl had estimated we would be at Camden Hall in time for dinner. Elisabeth was traveling in the coach with the earl's valet; the earl and I were riding.

We set off on time. Alonzo ignored the strange chestnut gelding trotting beside him through the busy London streets. Alonzo was very good about being in company with other horses. The circus had so many different horses, many coming and going, that he paid little attention to strangers. He knew he was the king, all of his human servants knew he was the king, and that was enough for him. He felt no need to assert his preeminence unless he was challenged. Which had never happened.

The earl's tall chestnut thoroughbred was not as comfortable with Alonzo as Alonzo was with him. The chestnut was a gelding and Alonzo was a stallion. The chestnut knew immediately that Alonzo was the king, and he kept trying to move sideways away from us. The earl handled him beautifully. I was impressed.

"What's his name?" I asked.

"Walter," he replied.

"*Walter*? That's a terrible name for such a beautiful animal."

"I know." The earl shot me a glance. "When he was born I made the mistake of telling my nephew he could name him. That is the name he chose. Don't ask me why—none of us could figure it out. But Walter it had to be. I had given him my word."

"How tall is he?" I asked the earl. Walter and the earl towered over Alonzo and me.

"Sixteen hands, two inches," he replied.

"Alonzo is fifteen hands, two inches," I said.

The earl said, "He looks bigger when you see him performing. He's so dominating. One simply can't take one's eyes off him. When you brought him to Grosvenor Square, I was surprised he was so small."

Small? Alonzo? I was annoyed at the very suggestion. "Fifteen-two is exactly the right size for an Andalusian stallion. You are just accustomed to that big thoroughbred you're riding. But Walter could never do what Alonzo does."

"That is true," the earl replied serenely, ignoring my annoyance. "Thoroughbreds are built to run, so their legs push out behind. Alonzo's hind legs are built to come under him, for collection." He looked over at Alonzo, who was trotting forward with a springy stride. "I thought he might be an Andalusian."

"He is a full-blooded Andalusian," I said proudly.

"They are very rare in England. I have only seen pictures."

"The Spanish are very jealous of their horses; they don't like to send them out of the country."

"How did you get him?"

I wasn't about to tell this stranger the story of how I got Alonzo, so I answered breezily, "I was lucky."

He recognized the snub and fell quiet. Except for a few observations about the countryside, we maintained the quiet for several hours.

*

The only part of England I had seen thus far had been the road from Dover, where we landed, to London. The ride to the earl's home in Berkshire afforded me a better opportunity to view the countryside. It was spring, my favorite time of year, and the world was in bloom. The new leaves were a light fresh green and the hedgerows along the road were darker than the lush grass. A soft warm wind was blowing, and I took my hat off so I could feel it blowing through my hair.

I lifted my face to the sun and the breeze and suddenly I found myself longing with all my heart to be riding through the French countryside with Papa and the circus. Tears stung behind my eyes and I blinked them away.

"England is at its most beautiful in the springtime," the earl said. We had been speaking English since the beginning of our journey.

"So is France," I replied, looking straight ahead so he wouldn't see my tears. "I love traveling in the spring. The horses are fresh from the winter's rest, and the whole circus feels alive and anxious to get to work again."

"What kind of acts do you have in your circus?" he asked.

The tears were gone and it was safe to look at him. Under the sun his hair was a halo of gold and his eyes were as clear a blue as the cloudless sky. He really was a splendid-looking man.

"It is mostly equestrian, of course," I answered. That's why we call it *Le Cirque Equestre*. We have horses that can do amusing tricks—the audience always likes that. *Maman* had a horse she trained to count—he could count up to forty!"

I glanced at him to see his reaction. "Forty?" he said. "Really?"

"Really."

"Do you still have him?"

"No." I sat very straight in the saddle and looked directly ahead. "When *Maman* died he wouldn't perform for anyone else. We kept him, of course, but he was old by then, and he missed *Maman*. He lasted only a year after she went."

"How old were you when your mother died?" he asked quietly.

"Thirteen." I turned to him, pleased that he had recognized *Maman* as my mother. "We have other acts. We have girls in beautiful costumes who stand on horseback as the horses canter around the ring; we have an acrobat who does somersaults on a cantering horse. We have Jojo and his horse who do a really funny act." I smiled thinking of it. "And, of course, we have Alonzo. He does a mirror ride with one of our other horses and he also performs the ride you saw at Astley's. Aside from the horses, we have dancing dogs, a really great magician, a very good high wire act, tumblers, a juggler, and a few other acts that vary from season to season. We also offer pony rides to the children before and after the show. I am always surprised how many children have never had the chance to sit on a horse."

I had continued to look forward as I spoke, but now I glanced at the man riding next to me, curious to see how he reacted to my list.

As if he felt my eyes, he turned his head to smile at me. "I have nephews who would love to see your circus. In fact, I would like to see it myself — especially the equestrian part. Is a mirror ride when horses do exactly the same thing at the same time to music?"

I nodded, pleased he knew what a mirror ride was. "Yes. Papa has a very nice horse that can do the lower-level movements. He is a Barb, not an Andalusian, but he does very well."

We had been riding for several hours when the earl asked me if I wanted to stop. I told him I wasn't tired, but I would like to eat something, and I would also like to offer Alonzo some hay and water.

Fifteen minutes later we pulled up in front of a coaching inn. When we were on the road in France we never went to the big inns—they were too expensive. We usually just pulled off the road and fed and watered our performers and horses ourselves.

The carriage horses passed under a big arch that led into a central courtyard and we followed. The inn, a large wooden building, stood on the right side of the courtyard and a few smaller buildings were on the left. Directly in front of us I saw a large stable.

Grooms were already at the heads of the carriage horses and another groom came running up to us. We dismounted and the earl gave directions that the horses were to be fed and watered. Two other men in the courtyard, who had been deserted by the grooms when the earl's carriage came in, stood with their horses patiently waiting. An earl took precedence, even in a coaching stableyard, I thought with disapproval. It had been like that in France before the revolution.

I took Elisabeth's hand and told her she was to come with us into the inn, and the earl said the same to his valet. As soon as we set foot inside, a man dressed in a leather waistcoat came rushing up to the earl. "My lord!" he gushed. "How nice to see you again! What can we do for you today?"

The earl bestowed a friendly smile upon the underling, who turned out to be the inn's owner. "I have a small party with me today, Charles, and I would like the private parlor."

"Certainly, certainly, my lord. It is always available for you. If you would just follow me."

The inn had a scuffed wood floor, a huge fireplace, a busy taproom, and a shop that was selling food. I caught the scent of chicken pie and my mouth watered. People were eating at wooden tables and benches. A few men holding large tankards were sitting in comfortable chairs in front of a huge fire.

We were escorted up a flight of stairs and into a small room where a fire was going in a stone fireplace. There was a table set with a white tablecloth and blue china in front of the fireplace. Chairs were set around it. It looked considerably more comfortable than the wooden tables and chairs downstairs.

What if this nice little room had already been taken I wondered. Would the innkeeper have evicted the occupants so he could accommodate an earl? Probably, I thought. The aristocracy reigned in England.

The earl directed Elisabeth and me to the necessaries room. "Good heavens," Elisabeth said as we stood together in front of a small mirror. "What did you do to your hair Isabel?"

My hair, which had been neatly tucked into a bun at the back of my head when we started, had come loose, and long strands decorated my neck and shoulders.

"I took my hat off for a while," I confessed.

"Let me fix it." She took a comb from her purse and pulled the whole bun apart. Then she combed everything back smoothly and tied it at my nape with a ribbon she also pulled from her purse. "There, that is better."

I looked in the mirror. It was much neater, and I smiled at her. "Thank you, Lisa," I said. It was my name for her.

"This earl, he treats you well? He does not say anything inappropriate?"

Elisabeth always fancied that any man we did not know would say inappropriate things to me.

"He was a perfect gentleman," I assured her. "How did you fare with the valet?"

She sniffed. "He thinks himself above me. I ignore him and look out the window. The countryside is more beautiful in France."

I agreed with her and we returned to the private room together, a solid French front against these English men.

Chapter Five

The food served at the inn was terrible: overcooked beef in heavy gravy with lumpy mashed potatoes. Elisabeth and I looked at each other and attempted to eat some of the dreadful stuff to be polite. When the earl remarked upon how little we had eaten, we assured him we were not very hungry. In fact, I was starving. I devoutly hoped the food at Camden Hall would be better.

As we rode along, getting ever closer to my temporary home, I thought with resignation that I had better learn something about the earl's family if I was going to be spending six months among them.

"This countess I resemble," I said as our horses trotted easily beside each other. "How exactly is she related to me?"

He gave me a pleased look. "She is your great-grandmother. She lived during the period of the first two Georges, and she managed to acquire a great deal of power by making herself the personal friend of both their queens. She was married to our great grandfather, the third earl, who was happy to remain at home in Camden Hall raising roses and building additions to the house. His great contribution to the family was to sire an heir, who became your grandfather—and mine as well.

I thought about this. "Then that makes you my first cousin."

"It does indeed," he replied cordially.

"And my moth…Maria…is your aunt?"

"Yes."

"Who is the aunt you said was living in your house?"

"Augusta. She was my grandfather's sister. She is also your aunt—great-aunt to be precise. She never married, which is why she lives at Camden Hall."

"But you own it."

"Not precisely. It is mine while I live, but I only hold it in trust for future generations. Whoever is the present earl is the head of the entire Sommer family, and I am happy to offer a home to my Aunt Augusta."

I thought about this, creating a sort of family tree in my mind. "Are there any other aunts or uncles I should know about?"

"There is Aunt Jane, who is the youngest and the most fun. She has a daughter who is your age and we must arrange for the two of you to meet. As for uncles—my father would have been your uncle, but he is dead, as are his two brothers. The women in my family appear to be longer lived than the men.

"Hmm." This collection of aunts and possible cousins did not make me feel comfortable, and I lapsed into silence for the rest of the ride.

*

We approached Camden Hall along a drive rimmed with beautiful tall oak trees just coming into leaf. The sun was setting in the west and when the house came into view, I must confess my breath caught in my throat. It was as magnificent as any French royal chateau, and it glowed in the dying sunlight like a jewel. A tree-lined lake formed part of the park-like grounds, and I saw a small herd of deer drinking from its gold-stained water. Behind it rose what the earl had told me were the Lambourn downs.

He was looking at me, waiting for a comment. I said honestly, "It's beautiful. It looks like a palace."

His smile revealed his pleasure at my response. He said, "The man who built it—the fourth earl—*thought* he was royalty. He was so arrogant and insufferable that he became known as the Proud Earl. When he inherited the house that was a mixture of Elizabethan and Jacobean styles, it didn't begin to live up to his standard. So he had a whole new house, in the style of a grand baroque palace, built on the front of the old."

"It looks a bit like Versailles," I ventured. Papa had taken me to look at Versailles one time when the circus was in winter recess.

"He would have been delighted to hear you say so. Versailles was his ideal."

I didn't say anything else. I just wondered how on earth I was going to endure life in this palace. Our house in the south of France was an old stone farmhouse with a sitting room, a large kitchen where we ate, and three bedrooms. The reason Papa had bought the house was that it came with 50 acres of property. He had renovated the stable and built large paddocks, one for Alonzo and one for his horse, Henri. The rest of our horses—my old pony, my riding horse, our driving horses, Papa's riding horse, and some horses from the circus—lived in a large open barn where they were fed and where they slept if the weather was bad. The winter was the time for them to get away from performing and just be horses.

I loved our house. I liked being close to the earth and close to the horses. I liked our small town, where everyone knew me. I loved the traveling with the circus, but the winter in our snug little home was also a time I treasured.

I was quiet as the earl and I rode up to the front of the palace. The carriage, which had kept pace with us all along, pulled up behind us. The earl dismounted, as did I. The palace's magnificent door had opened and a tall man in a formal black coat and pants came down the front steps. I didn't budge from my position next to Alonzo. The earl looked at me, then motioned to the butler (I assumed he was a butler; he looked the part). The butler came down the path and gave a small bow to the earl. "Welcome home, my lord," he said.

"Thank you, Hobbs." The earl didn't appear at all discomposed by my behavior. "This is my cousin, Lady Isabel. She has come for a visit of some months."

The tall man bowed to me. "Welcome to Camden Hall, my lady. I am his lordship's butler, Hobbs. Should you ever need anything you must come to me."

"Thank you," I said in a stifled voice.

We moved out of the way as the coach drew up. When Elisabeth came down the steps I wanted to run and hide my face between her breasts the way I had done after *Maman* died. I stiffened my back.

The earl said, "Did you get my message about where to put Lady Isabel's maid?"

Before the butler could answer I said to the earl, "Elisabeth is not my maid! She is my friend!"

"I beg your pardon, Isabel," he returned. "I did not mean to insult her."

Before I could answer an elderly man came up to me and said, "I will take the horse to the stable, my lady."

I tightened my hand on the reins. "There is no need. I can see to my own horse—if you would just point the way to the stable?"

Catastrophic silence.

The earl said in his calm, pleasant voice, "Isabel, you can safely trust Alonzo to Stoddard. He is my Head Groom and has forgot more about horses than I ever knew."

I stiffened. It was starting. They were trying to take Alonzo away from me. "He does not know Alonzo," I said fiercely.

Alonzo, meanwhile, had decided he was weary and rested his heavy head on my shoulder. The groom smiled. "I can see he is attached to you, my lady. But all we will do is rub him down and put him in a nice big stall with some grain and hay. He'll be just fine for the night, and tomorrow you can tell me all about him."

Alonzo removed his head and gazed at the house, as if fascinated. This was a battle I could not win. Alonzo had been perfectly fine in the earl's London stable for a night; he would be perfectly fine here. It was I who was not fine.

"Very well," I said stiffly. I made myself hand the reins to the earl's Head Groom and allowed the earl to escort me to the huge carved wood front door of this much too big house. Elisabeth trailed behind us, holding a cloth traveling bag. The earl's valet came after her.

I passed through the door into a coldly formal hall with a floor of black and white squares. The earl slipped his hand under my elbow and walked me down the hall, speaking casually about some of the priceless items—statues, urns, paintings—that lined the walls on either side. I caught glimpses of fabulously decorated rooms opening off the hall, rooms the earl casually described as the "Blue Salon," "The Green Salon," "The Morning Room," as we went by. We finally stopped at the bottom of a magnificent double staircase, where a stout, gray-haired woman awaited us.

The earl said, "Isabel, this is my housekeeper, Mrs. Ann Adams. She will show you and Elisabeth to your rooms." He gave me a reassuring smile. "Mrs. Adams will send someone to help you find your way to the dining room. I expect you'll want to freshen up and change your clothes. Can you be ready for dinner in half an hour or would you like more time?"

I was starving and could be ready for dinner in fifteen minutes, but I said instead, "Where is Elisabeth to eat?"

"I am hoping Mademoiselle Lagasse will join me in the housekeeper's rooms for dinner," Mrs. Adams said, sending a smile Elisabeth's way.

Elisabeth's English was rudimentary, but she understood what the housekeeper was saying and said politely, "Merci, Madame."

Elisabeth and I followed the housekeeper up two flights of carpeted stairs then down a wide carpeted corridor until she stopped, opened a door, and gestured for me to precede her.

The bedroom was huge. The windows were hung with heavy crimson curtains, which were open so the light of the setting sun came into the room. A great four-poster bed was hung with the same crimson material as the curtains, and the pale gold paper on the walls had Chinese pagodas engraved on it. Papa and I could have fit our whole house into this room.

I walked to one of the windows, looked out and saw a stag drinking out of the lake, his antlers silhouetted against the red-gold sky. It was beautiful.

The housekeeper had walked to a door in one of the walls and, as I turned, she opened it, smiled at me and said, "The earl requested I put you in the Red Room, Lady Isabel, so your maid could sleep in the attached dressing room."

I was relieved to know Elisabeth would be so close to me, and we both went to inspect her new quarters.

The dressing room was bigger than our sitting room at home. It held a bed, a table with a washbasin, a dresser, a big mirror and a rack for hanging clothes. I looked over my shoulder at Elisabeth and said in French, "What do you think, Lisa?"

"I like it," she replied.

I smiled at the housekeeper. "Thank you, Mrs. Adams. This will do nicely."

The woman nodded. Her gray hair was neatly parted in the middle and pulled back into a bun. She was one of those women who could have been anything from 40 to 60. She had a pleasant face with a small nose and kind brown eyes.

She said, "In half an hour a footman will come to show Lady Isabel to the drawing room and Miss Lagasse to my rooms. I will leave you now to tidy up."

I said, "Thank you," and Elisabeth said, *"Merci."*

The housekeeper led us back into my bedroom then turned to face me. Her smile was a benediction. "Welcome home, my lady," she said. "We are all so very glad to see you."

I didn't answer. I couldn't answer. This wasn't my home. It would never be my home. I managed a nod and she closed the door behind her.

*

Both our bags were delivered before Mrs. Adams was all the way down the hall. Other than riding clothes, my wardrobe was minimal. We didn't live the sort of life that called for a lot of changes of clothes. I did have two nice dresses, which I wore to church. I decided on the blue muslin, and Elisabeth fastened the back for me. There was a cheval mirror in the room, and I went to take a look.

As the dress was for church, it had a modest neckline and sleeves. The soft material was gathered under my breasts and fell to the tops of my shoes in simple but graceful folds. I never wore any jewelry; we spent our money on horses. Elisabeth had just told me to sit in front of the dressing table when a knock sounded on the door. She went to answer it and I heard a male voice say, "I am to escort Lady Isabel to the dining room and Miss Lagasse to Mrs. Adams."

Elisabeth's English was good enough to understand this and she said, "You wait. We come."

"Certainly," the voice said. "I'll be right outside."

Elisabeth closed the door and almost ran over to where I was still seated. "We will have to do it *a la jeune fille*," she said. "There is no time for a fashionable chignon."

"Just do it the way you do when I am performing," I said soothingly. "That takes no time at all."

She muttered something under her breath and picked up the hairbrush she had unpacked from the bag she was carrying. She brushed out my hair and pulled it back into a simple bun on the nape of my neck. It looked fine and so I told her.

I stood up, drew a long breath, and we went to the door.

A footman dressed in blue and silver livery awaited us, and we followed him down the stairs. At the bottom we turned left then stopped in front of a very large room that I saw had paintings on the ceiling. "This is the drawing room, my lady," the footman said. He waited for me to go in.

A lump of anxiety was knotting my stomach, and I was angry with myself for feeling nervous. What did I care what these people thought of me? This was not my world. It would never be my world. I would stay for the time Papa had agreed to and then I would go back to France where I belonged. I stuck my chin in the air and walked into the room.

Chapter Six

I flicked my eyes quickly around the huge room and was stunned by the impression of enormous wealth. A group of people were gathered around an enormous marble chimney piece and I stepped onto the room's thick carpet and walked slowly in their direction. Everyone's head turned at the same time to look at me.

The earl had been standing in front of the fireplace and he covered the ground between us with long strides. "Isabel," he said with a smile that would melt lead. "Come and allow me to introduce you."

He was wearing a black coat with tails, buff knee breeches, white stockings and black shoes. He looked very different from the man I had ridden with all day, which didn't help my nervousness.

Instead of taking my arm, he took my hand in his large, warm grasp and led me across miles of carpet to the fireplace. I curled my fingers around his so he wouldn't desert me. At last we reached the circle of uncomfortable-looking gilt chairs occupied by people dressed as if they expected to go to a ball. The elderly woman, whom I supposed must be the great aunt the earl had told me of, glanced from me, to the portrait over the chimneypiece, then back to me again. I looked at the picture myself.

It was the same one the earl had showed Papa and me in London. He must have had it sent back here. I stared once again at the gray-eyed woman in the portrait. Her face might have my eyes and features, but there was an air of arrogance, of superiority, about this woman, an air that the world was hers for the taking. I looked at this proof of my ancestry and wanted to take a knife to it.

"You could have sat for that portrait," someone said, and I tore my eyes away from the portrait that had destroyed my life.

The earl said, "Aunt Augusta, may I present Lady Isabel Lewins." He looked down at me and said in a gentle voice, "Lady Augusta is your mother's aunt, Isabel. She is your great-aunt."

He squeezed my hand lightly, dropped it and motioned me forward with his eyes. I went to stand before the woman who was sitting ramrod straight in the gilt chair closest to the lit fire, thought briefly that perhaps I should curtsey, banished the notion and instead held out my hand and said steadily, "How do you do."

She took my hand and held it between her vein-ridged old ones. "Dear God," she said in a shaking voice. She looked at the earl. "I didn't know if I should believe you, Leo, when you wrote you had found Maria's lost child. But she is the exact image of Beatrice." She turned back to me and said in a voice that trembled, "Welcome home, my child. Welcome home!"

A short silence fell. She was probably waiting for me to say I was happy to be here. But I wasn't happy to be here, and I wasn't going to say I was.

The earl said smoothly, "And this is my brother, Robert Sommer, and his wife, Margaret."

I offered my hand to Robert Sommer, who had stood when I came in. He was a pale replica of his brother, with hair so blond it was almost white, and light blue eyes. His smile looked warm and genuine as he greeted me.

"How do you do," I said again.

Margaret Sommer was a beauty with red-gold hair and green eyes. She greeted me politely and I made a polite reply.

Next came Roger Lavery, the earl's cousin. According to the earl, he had gambled away all his money and was living at Camden Hall because he had nowhere else to go. He had dark red hair with a foxlike face to match. He looked me up and down, smiled and said, "So pleased to meet you, Cousin. I hope we're going to be friends."

I had seen that sort of look before and I narrowed my eyes.

A bell sounded from the doorway, saving me the necessity of replying, and I turned to see Hobbs standing there. "Dinner is served, my lord," he intoned in a voice so deep and solemn he might have been announcing the Pope.

Everyone stood up.

Aunt Augusta said, "I think it would be appropriate for you to take Isabel in, Leo."

His name was Leo. *Leo the lion*, I thought. The name was appropriate.

He said, "How thoughtful, Aunt Augusta," then, to his brother, "Rob, will you take Aunt Augusta in?"

"Of course."

The earl took my arm, and to my astonishment, we proceeded to line up as if we were in a parade. We actually did parade into the dining room, where filled soup plates had already been placed on a magnificent mahogany table. The earl escorted me to the seat on his right, and Lady Augusta sat across from me. Robert and his wife sat across from each other and Roger sat alone. Hobbs was posted next to a side table that held decanters of wine, and two footmen stood with him.

Did they do this every night? Everyone was beautifully dressed, the men in perfectly cut black evening clothes and Aunts Augusta and Margaret in dresses that put my simple blue muslin to shame. The footmen were resplendent in satin livery and white wigs. I looked at the soup that was sitting in front of me and my stomach quivered with hunger. I picked up my spoon.

The soup was broth. It was also thin, tasteless and lukewarm. I wondered how long it had sat on the table waiting for us to parade in. I managed a few sips. At home our soup is hearty and always, always hot. Nobody I knew would dream of serving lukewarm soup.

One of the footmen left his post to remove the soup plates from the table. The second footman took a platter of food from a third footman who had brought it from the kitchen, or so I supposed.

Footman number two was circling the table, offering the platter to each of the diners. I took a piece off the platter planning to ask for more if I liked it, and when I inspected it more closely, I saw it was fish. I love fish. I took a bite. It was overcooked. I took two tiny bites to be polite and waited patiently until the appropriate footman came and took it away.

The vegetables were on the table and when the earl held a bowl of carrots for me, I took them eagerly. My life might be in tatters, but I was hungry.

The carrots had been overcooked until there was virtually no taste left in them. The potatoes were better. It's hard to ruin potatoes.

The next course offered by one of the footman was a plate of cutlets. I shook my head. I had no idea what they were, and I wasn't inclined to find out.

After the cutlets had been removed, another footman placed a large roasted turkey in front of the earl. I could feel myself perk up. I allowed the footman to place several slices on my plate and—to my astonishment—they were delicious. I ate them all and asked for more.

The earl, who had been keeping up a conversation with Lady Augusta, turned to me and said humorously, "Thank God you like something, Isabel."

It's the only food that's been properly cooked. I thought it but I didn't say it. I merely returned his smile and took another forkful of turkey.

Once the dessert had been served—a very good apple pie—the earl rose and said, "I believe that in honor of Isabel's arrival we should all return to the drawing room together."

I looked at him in bewilderment. Did the English usually go their separate ways after they ate their very formal meal? At home Papa and I gathered for dinner around our old dining room table in front of a roaring fire to eat the delicious cooking of our housekeeper, Estelle. We rarely ate alone. There was always someone from the circus visiting, and we talked over ideas for new acts and joked and laughed and drank wine and stayed at the table for hours. It was much nicer than this *tableau* the English performed at dinner. It was...home.

We all stood and suddenly I had had enough. I put my hand on the earl's sleeve and said, "My lord, will you mind if I retire? It has been a long day and I am tired."

"Of course, you must go to bed if you are tired, Isabel," he said immediately. "I know..." he frowned. "I know this isn't easy for you." His blue eyes suddenly glinted. "Would you like to go for a ride before breakfast tomorrow? I can show you around the park."

Would I like to get out of this house and into the open air? "Oh *yes*," I said. Then I remembered, and sadly shook my head. "I want to give Alonzo a day of rest after the long trip yesterday."

"Isabel." He held my eyes. "I have twenty horses eating their heads off in my stable. I'm sure we can find something for you to ride."

I felt tears sting behind my eyes. *This will not do.* I straightened my shoulders, thanked him, and agreed when he told me to meet him in the library at 7:00 a.m.

Chapter Seven

Elisabeth was waiting for me. She undid my dress, hung it in the mahogany wardrobe and brushed out my hair. Her touch was so loving, so maternal, that I almost begged her to sleep in the huge four-poster with me. There was certainly enough room for two people.

But I needed to be strong for the both of us, so I kissed her good night and watched as she disappeared through the door that led into her little room. I climbed into the big bed and thought with longing of my bed at home.

Everything in this house was alien. These people who were supposed to be my family, were total strangers. They lived a way of life I would never approve of or understand. At dinner Lady Augusta had spoke of presenting me to the Queen to *validate my social status*. What had she been talking about? I was a prisoner here for six months and then I was going home.

I was very tired, but I couldn't fall asleep. I lay in that big bed, in that huge room, listening to the silence of that enormous house. At home, if I were sleepless, I would go to the kitchen for a glass of warm milk. But here, in this huge palace, I was as trapped as a rabbit in a cage.

I must have fallen asleep eventually because I was awakened by the sound of my door opening. I sat up with a jerk, pulling the soft wool blanket up to my chin.

A girl in a maid's uniform was in my room. "I'm sorry if I startled you, Lady Isabel," she said, "but his lordship told me you were to go riding with him this morning."

The sun was coming up as I sorted through the things Elisabeth had unpacked yesterday. The maid turned from the fire she had been making up to say, "Do you need some help dressing, my lady?"

"No, thank you," I said. "If you have finished with the fire you may leave."

The maid jumped to her feet. "Of course, my lady. I didn't mean to be in your way."

She looked to be about my age, and I felt ashamed I had been so curt. "I'm sorry if I sounded abrupt," I said in my usual voice. "What is your name?"

"Mary Ann, my Lady. I will be making up your fire and cleaning your room."

I let out a long breath and said humorously, "Does that mean I don't have to make the bed myself?"

"No, no, Lady Isabel. I will make the bed for you!" Mary Ann looked absolutely horrified.

We chatted for a few more minutes, then she left and I began to dress in the riding clothes I had unearthed. I had put on my breeches and overskirt when Elisabeth's door opened and she came in.

"You should have waked me," she said reproachfully.

"Don't be silly. I can put on my own riding clothes."

She walked to the dressing table and picked up a brush. "Your hair has come out of its plait. Come, let me fix it for you."

Elisabeth smoothed out my hair then tied it at the nape of my neck with a blue ribbon.

I said, "I'm supposed to meet the earl in the library, but I don't know where it is."

"Someone will be downstairs to show you." She smiled, kissed me on the cheek and said, "Have a nice ride."

I grinned at her. The thought of going to the stables instead of meeting the family again had cheered me up.

A footman was in the hall downstairs and he was happy to escort me to the library, which lay off the hallway beyond the drawing room. When I peeked in from the hallway, I saw the first room in this enormous house that I liked. It actually looked comfortable. Cushioned sofas and chairs were scattered about, as were an assortment of various-size tables. A thick rug covered the floor, and shelves of books lined the walls.

The earl was standing behind a large desk looking down at a paper in his hand. His head lifted when I came in. I stopped in the center of the rug and turned in a slow pirouette, looking at the four book-lined walls. "Do you know how many books are here?"

"They number several thousand I believe."

"Goodness." I began to walk toward him. "I won't ask if you've read them all."

"Thank you," he returned emphatically. "Everyone else who comes in here for the first time always asks that question."

"And what do you answer?" I inquired.

"I always say that I have."

I laughed.

He came around the desk and looked me up and down. "I have to admit I wondered what kind of riding clothes you wore," he said. "I just couldn't see you in a sidesaddle."

I looked down at my outfit. In a show I always wore a uniform in the style of St. Cyr, but to ride out in public I wore men's breeches and high boots with a skirt over them. The skirt was split in the middle to accommodate my riding astride. It achieved modesty because it covered my legs.

I said, "To ride properly one has to have two legs on the horse. A whip cannot replace a leg."

"I agree. Come let's walk down to the stable. I told Stoddard to have Gypsy ready for you. She's a thoroughbred mare, and she can be a bit of a handful, but I think she'll behave for you. She's one of my favorite rides."

"If I am riding your mare, then who are you riding?"

"My old gray gelding, Silver Boy. He's almost twenty but he's perfectly healthy and I know he'll enjoy an outing."

We left the house and began to walk along a wide path that led through a flower garden that would be magnificent when all its buds burst into bloom. A stone fountain stood in its middle, with the statue of a maiden pouring water into an ewer. As the water overflowed the ewer it splashed into the fountain.

"I like your fountain," I said.

He looked down at me and grinned. "I do too. We have other fountains that are considered finer statuary, but I like the simplicity of this one."

He looked younger when he smiled like that. I wondered how old he was and so I asked.

"Very old," he returned gravely. "I turned thirty my last birthday."

He didn't look thirty to me. The sun had risen above the horizon and the morning sun was warm on my head. With his bright hair and intensely blue eyes, the earl looked like a Viking pirate. No wife had appeared at dinner last night and no one had spoken as if a wife existed. I briefly wondered why. He owned this vast estate. Wouldn't he want heirs to inherit it?

I was curious, but his marital status was not my business and I didn't ask.

*

The stables were a revelation. There were three separate buildings: one for the carriage horses, one for the riding horses and one for the farm horses. The earl took me into the riding horse barn, where Alonzo was housed.

Stoddard must have been looking for us for he appeared almost immediately. "Shall I have the horses saddled, my lord?" he asked.

"Yes. Lady Isabel and I are going to visit Alonzo first."

"How was he last night?" I asked the Head Groom. "Did he settle in?"

"He settled in like a champion, my lady. He stood quiet while we rubbed him down, and when we put him in his stall he ate every bit of his grain and hay. When I looked in on him at midnight he was stretched out on his side and snoring." He shook his head. "I never seen a stallion that calm."

"He's an Andalusian. They are known for their excellent temperament."

"Oh, that's what he is. I never saw a horse like him. Our thoroughbred stallions don't have that kind of muscle."

The earl asked, "Is Alonzo still in his stall or have you put him outside?"

"I kept him in just in case Lady Isabel wanted to see him before you rode out, my lord."

I beamed at Stoddard. "Thank you. I want to see him very much."

"Follow me, my lady."

The stable aisle was wide and immaculate. There was not a trace of hay or manure on the stone floor and the air smelled fresh and clean. Alonzo was at the end of the aisle, with an empty stall between him and the nearest horse. His stall had a double door with the bottom door closed and the top door latched open. I stepped close to the opening and said softly, *"Bonjour, mon ami.* You are behaving yourself I hear."

He had been hunting in his straw bedding for loose hay but at the sound of my voice his head shot up. He nickered, crossed the stall to push his nose into my outstretched hand, and nickered again. I kept my back to the two men, scratching my horse's face and behind his ears. There were tears in my eyes, and I didn't want them to see.

Stop being such a baby, I scolded myself. *Alonzo has traveled all his life. What made you think he would be unhappy in this beautiful stable?*

The earl said, "Stoddard and I will wait for you in the stableyard, Isabel. Come when you're ready."

Still with my back to him, I nodded. When they were gone, I began to talk to Alonzo.

Chapter Eight

The mare the earl gave me to ride was a beauty. Her bay coat shone like mahogany in the sunlight, and the arch of her neck was perfect. Stoddard stood at her head as we waited for the earl to mount.

"She can be tricky, my lady," he warned me. "But if you ride that stallion I reckon you can manage her."

"We'll be fine," I said with a smile.

The earl moved his horse up beside me and we walked out of the stableyard together. I looked at the horse he had chosen and smiled. He was lovely. His gray coat had turned pure white—as Alonzo's would when he grew old—but his ears were pricked, and he was prancing a little. He was clearly delighted to be going for a ride.

I said, "Did you choose to ride Silver Boy because he would be a settling influence on the mare?"

He laughed. "I see I'm caught out. Gypsy has a mind of her own. She's thrown just about everyone who ever rode her. But she respects Silver Boy."

"She'll respect me too," I said. Just as I finished my sentence a rabbit ran across our path. Gypsy took exception to this interloper and bucked. I pulled her head up, closed my legs around her and sent her forward. I felt her gathering for another buck and I closed my legs tighter. Her head came up in surprise and she scooted forward in a trot. I brought her back to a walk and waited for the earl to catch up.

"Thank you!" he said as Silver Boy came alongside of me. "I love this mare. She can jump over the moon if she wants to, but she's not calm enough to hunt."

"Is that what you want to do with her? Hunt?"

"It's why I bought her. She's big enough to carry me and she has enough bone to be a hunter. I just don't fancy being bucked off in front of all my friends."

"I've seen other horses like this. They're too smart for their own good. If they see a chance to take advantage, they will. Gypsy would probably do well as a hunter. It would keep her mind occupied."

The earl looked down at me in surprise. "Do you think she's *bored*?"

"Certainly she's bored. You English..." My voice trailed off. I didn't want to insult the man.

"What about the English?"

Well, he had asked me. "You don't know how to ride," I said bluntly.

We had been riding along a very pretty trail, which went through what the earl called the "Home Woods." Alonzo would enjoy such a ride; he would find it relaxing. But if all he did was walk trot and canter through the woods every day, he'd be bored to death. Alonzo liked to think.

I shared this thought with the earl. "He likes to think?" he repeated.

"He does. Most horses don't. They're happy if they are taken care of, fed, exercised and given a chance to be with other horses. But the special horse—the horse like Alonzo and, I believe, this mare—they get bored. And when they're bored they get up to all sorts of tricks—like throwing their riders."

We were trotting side by side as we spoke, and now we came out of the woods into an open pasture. "Care for a gallop?" the earl said.

My answer was to send Gypsy forward. I had never before ridden a thoroughbred at the gallop and it was wonderful. Gypsy was young and healthy and bred to run. She told me through the reins how happy she was. I gathered her a little, so she was in better balance, and she gave to me. When we had reached the woods on the far side of the pasture we pulled up. I patted her neck and told her what a good girl she was. She was very pleased with herself.

The earl and Silver Boy arrived. Silver Boy was breathing normally, and I gave full credit to the earl for keeping his horses in good condition. Gypsy began to sidle around. She wanted to gallop again. I said, "She doesn't know how to yield to the leg. I could teach her that if you like. Right now all she knows what to do when you put your leg on her is to go forward."

He said, "If she's going to be a hunter, isn't that all she needs to know?"

I shook my head. "You need to have control of your horse's hindquarters if you're going to be safe.'"

"If you'd like to work with her, I would be most appreciative," he said. "The hunting season starts in December and I really would like to hunt Gypsy."

I had been worried about what I was going to find to do in this place and now I had something. I beamed at him and said, "I would love to."

*

We galloped some more and then the earl led us to a lovely little *clairiere*—he called it a "glade." It was a grassy open space on the river that ran through the earl's property. By this time even Gypsy was willing to stop and graze for a while.

The earl and I sat comfortably on the new grass. The early sunlight filtered through the subtly greening branches of the trees and the earl picked up a stone that was near to him and threw it into the river making it skip.

And that single movement—the image of his arm arching to release the stone, of his eyes intently following the arc of the stone as it landed, his look of satisfaction when it skipped four times—the Earl of Camden became a real person to me. He might be an earl, he might be rich, he might wield enormous power, but he threw stones into the river just like every other boy or man I ever knew. I laughed.

"What's so funny?" he asked.

He had stretched out on the grass, leaning up on his elbow so he could face me. The sun slanting from the east shone on his hair and face. "I have a favor to ask of you Isabel," he said.

I tilted my head in inquiry. "What favor?"

"I would like it very much if you would stop calling me 'my lord,' and start calling me 'Leo.'"

"Aunt Augusta calls you 'Camden.'"

"Sometimes, when she is being very correct. My brother, my sister-in-law, my nephews and my cousin Roger all call me Leo. I should like you to join them."

"I suppose I can do that," I said carefully.

He smiled at me. He had to know the power of that smile. "Thank you, Isabel," he said.

I said, "You're welcome," and didn't smile back.

*

We left the horses off at the stable and returned to the house for breakfast. As we reached the room that Leo called the breakfast room, we saw Aunt Augusta coming slowly down the stairs. We waited for her, and when she reached the bottom she stared at me in horror. "What is that extraordinary outfit you are wearing?" she demanded.

"I am wearing my riding clothes," I replied calmly. "Leo and I went for a ride before breakfast."

Aunt Augusta said to Leo, "I have been thanking God she speaks English as we do, even if she does have an unfortunate French accent. Imagine if she had learned from some low-class person who lived in a place like *Yorkshire*." She shuddered at the very thought.

Both Papa and I learned English from a young man who had helped with the circus horses one season. Jamie had told us he was the third son of a well-off family and his father had tried to push him into the church. He had wanted to go into the army, but his father wouldn't buy him a commission. So he ran away and joined our circus. He remained with us over the winter, but Papa wouldn't let him come on tour with us again. He said Jamie was too interested in me. I had liked him, and I missed the opportunity to practice my English.

Aunt Augusta followed up her statement about my English with further words about my person, "We must get this poor child some proper clothing immediately. She cannot meet people looking as she does now."

I looked at her steadily and said, "My clothing is perfectly respectable. I don't mind adding a few items to my wardrobe, but this is what I wear when I ride. I will never wear one of those voluminous skirts aristocratic women are swathed in when they ride sidesaddle."

Aunt Augusta's nose quivered. "Camden," she said. "Will you please talk some sense into this chit?"

Leo replied in a voice that might sound pleasant but was unmistakably the voice of authority. "Isabel is a brilliant rider, Aunt Augusta. If these are the clothes she wishes to wear while she is in the saddle, then she will wear them. However, I do agree that she needs a new wardrobe. I was wondering if Aunt Jane might be persuaded to take her shopping. I believe Susan will be making her come-out this year. The girls might enjoy each other's company."

Aunt Augusta's nostrils flared, and her nose quivered even more. "Very well, Camden," she said stiffly. "If that is what you wish."

"It is." He treated her to his beguiling smile. "I know your sensibilities are outraged, Aunt, but anyone who sees Isabel ride will understand. Now, come along and let us have breakfast."

The old lady melted. I suspected Leo usually got the result he wanted with that smile. I suspected that he knew it too.

"Very well," Aunt Augusta replied. She turned to me, a stern look on her face, and said, "I am certain that Isabel will prefer to change before she joins us."

She didn't suggest that Leo change from his riding clothes, but I refrained from pointing that out and agreed with her. It made no sense to ruffle Aunt Augusta's feathers any more than they already were. I had agreed to live here for six months and it would be idiotic to alienate the people I had to share the house with.

*

I changed into the rust-colored day dress our local seamstress had made. Elisabeth brushed out my hair, wound it into a bun on the nape of my neck, and I went downstairs to eat.

The breakfast room had added two more people, Leo's brother Robert and his wife Margaret. Margaret saw me first and said, "Breakfast is on the side table, Isabel. Help yourself."

I was expecting to see *baguettes, croissants, brioche,* perhaps even *pain au chocolate.* But there was food on the table. Real food, like ham, bacon, kidneys, smoked fish. The thought of eating meat for breakfast made my stomach turn. I put a boiled egg and 2 muffins on my plate and took a seat next to Margaret.

Robert was talking to Leo about a repair on the estate and Aunt Augusta was listening, so Margaret turned to me and said pleasantly, "I hear you and Leo went for a ride this morning, Isabel."

I swallowed the piece of muffin in my mouth and replied, "Yes, we did. The property is beautiful."

Margaret smiled faintly. "Camden Hall has over 7,000 acres, and 2,300 tenants farm the land. My husband manages the estate for his brother."

I had taken another bite of muffin and had to chew it and swallow before I could speak again. Margaret turned her face back to the table and picked up her cup. Her profile was perfect. She was a very beautiful woman. I wondered why she had married the brother and not the earl.

Her family probably weren't good enough, I thought cynically. We French are very pragmatic about such things. Rank counts even on the village level. The baker's daughter could never marry the son of the local landowner. She wouldn't have enough to offer her new family.

"I understand you have two sons," I said when I had finished chewing.

She turned to me and smiled radiantly. She was really gorgeous. "Yes, we do. David is ten and Charles is eight. They will be coming home from Eton for the summer. I cannot wait to see them."

"Is this Eton a school?"

She lifted her chin a fraction of an inch. "It is the finest school in England. Only boys from the very best families are accepted there. David is Leo's heir, so of course he had to go to Eton. And Charles naturally followed his brother."

"They do not live at home? But they are only ten and eight. Is that not *difficile* for them?"

"Oh, they are homesick at first, of course. But they soon adjust."

"And you? Do you miss them?"

"Of course I do," she retorted. "What kind of mother do you think I am?"

I drew back in my chair. "I'm sorry. I'm sure you're a very good mother. I never meant to suggest otherwise."

There was a short silence, then she gave me a repentant smile. "I didn't mean to snap at you, Isabel. It's just that I miss them very much and it hurt that you thought I might feel otherwise."

I returned her smile. "I understand. I am looking forward to meeting them."

We both returned to our breakfasts.

Chapter Nine

My first weeks at Camden Hall were horrid. The family might have been speaking Russian for all the sense they made to me. I tried my best to hide my feelings and act like the polite, accommodating girl I had promised Papa I would be. But alone in my room at night I had such an ache of emptiness in my heart that I thought I might die of it. I hated this huge house. I hated the dreadful food. I hated Aunt Augusta for wanting to turn me into an English lady. The only thing that kept me in England was the thought of the money that would ensure Papa's future. I couldn't remember a time when we had not been together, and his absence was a constant ache in my heart.

On my first day at Camden, Aunt Augusta had taken me on a tour of the house. It took hours, and by the time she was finished my head was reeling with the names of all of the priceless paintings and sculptures and furniture I had seen. I liked what I had seen of the medieval part of the house, with its crooked layout and small rooms, far better than I liked the magnificence of the new part.

Leo asked me if I enjoyed Aunt Augusta's tour and I had said what I thought: "It isn't right that one man should own so much when so many people are going hungry."

"I don't own it, Isabel. I am only keeping it in trust for the next generation."

"Of your family."

"Yes. Of my family."

"If you lived in France you would have had your head cut off."

"I probably would have," he agreed amiably. "Fortunately, however, I do not live in France. I live in England, and I can assure you that not a single man, woman or child who lives on my property is starving."

I shrugged. "You asked for my opinion."

"And now I have it," he replied, and changed the subject. "I know you must be homesick. Is there anything I can do to make this transition easier for you?"

I had an immediate answer to this question. "I would very much like to have a room that can be for only me and Elisabeth. A little parlor will do. In the old side of the house preferably. Everywhere we go in the big house it seems we meet a family member. We have to stay in my bedroom if we want to talk or read."

Two days after this discussion Leo showed me a lovely room in the medieval part of the house. The walls were painted pale yellow and it had a westerly view from its two windows so I could see the lake. It was also big enough to hold a sofa, several comfortable chairs, two bookcases, a desk and a table. The rug on the floor was old, but still thick enough to warm up the room. The fireplace was made of brick.

"It's yours, Isabel," Leo said. "For you and Elisabeth. I will make it clear to the family that they are not to disturb you unless they have been invited."

It was really Aunt Augusta and Roger I needed to avoid. I rarely saw Robert or Margaret except at dinnertime. Robert had an office in the house but was often out on the property. I had no idea where Margaret hid herself during the day. Aunt Augusta, on the other hand, was omnipresent, and Roger always seemed to appear when I least expected him. I didn't like Roger. I didn't like the way he looked at me, and I didn't like the way he called me "Circus Girl" when we were alone.

*

My first month at Camden went by and I was surprised to find myself too busy to think about my enforced exile. I rode with Leo in the morning, spent time with Elisabeth in my new sitting room, wrote long letters to Papa, did some reading, went back to the stable in the afternoon and worked with Leo on his seat and aids.

He was a quick student. It helped that he had a better seat than most of the English riders I had seen, and his hands were light. We worked in an outdoor ring that Leo had caused to be created with the dimensions of a French ménage, which is always an indoor ring.

On a day I will never forget Leo and I were working in the ring. Leo was riding Alonzo and I was offering advice. "That's better," I called as they came down the long line of the ring. "Try to keep your back supple. Don't stiffen up. Thighs flat against the saddle. Good, yes—that's it. Now bring him to a halt."

Alonzo halted. "Very nice," I said as Leo gave Alonzo more rein and walked him toward me. It had been cloudy all day, but at that moment the sun burst through. The brilliant light made Alonzo's coat shine like silver and illuminated Leo's bright hair and the splendid bone structure of his face. I thought that the two together looked as if they could conquer the world.

They pulled up in front of me and Leo grinned. His eyes were shining like twin sapphires. He said, "He's wonderful."

I smiled back. It was impossible not to. "You kept your base better this time. Everything in classical equitation—and I mean everything—depends upon the seat."

His eyes grew even bluer. "A word of praise from Isabel. I'm inspired."

I went to Alonzo's head and ignored his rider. "You are such a good boy to put up with a beginner on your back," I said, rubbing his face.

Alonzo blew out through his nose.

Leo dismounted. "I have always been accounted an excellent rider. I think you could have more sympathy for my self-esteem, Isabel."

"Your self-esteem needs no help from me," I told him tartly. "Everyone on this estate thinks you're just one step down from God."

"But you don't think that."

"Certainly not," I said. I handed him Alonzo's reins. "I need to work him for a little," I said as I ran up the stirrup to fit my height.

"Go ahead," he said equably. "I'll watch."

*

I rode for a half hour then Leo and I returned Alonzo to the stable where he would be brushed and put out in his grassy paddock until it was time for his dinner. As we walked toward the house Leo said casually, as if he were not imparting any news of note, "I heard from your mother this morning. She has arrived home from a visit in Ireland and only just got my letter about you. She will be here on Friday."

My stomach contracted and my heart beat faster. Leo had told me about my mother's absence from England and I had deliberately put her out of my mind. This news was not welcome.

Leo stopped walking and I stopped as well. I looked up at him and lifted my eyebrows in inquiry.

"Isabel." The way he said my name was different and it put me on guard. "Why don't you want to meet your mother?"

I parried. "Why should you think I don't want to meet her?"

"Because you freeze up every time I mention her."

I started walking, my back and shoulders stiff with resistance. How could I tell him how I really felt—that if I were nice to this other mother, I would be betraying my mother in heaven.

He caught me up and walked beside me, shortening his long gait to suit mine. I said, without looking at him, "I already have a mother. I don't need another one."

"Ah," he said. "So that is it."

"Yes, that is it," I snapped back.

We walked a few more steps then he put his hand on my arm and forced me turn to face him. I wanted to pull away, but his blue stare held me in place. In a quiet level voice he said, "This meeting isn't about you, Isabel. It's about Maria. After nineteen years of agonizing about what might have befallen her stolen baby, she deserves to know you are well and that your life has been a happy one." He tightened his grip on my arm, "Why can't you understand that? You could have been sold to the worst sort of people. You could have spent your life working yourself to death in a slum. You could have been pushed into prostitution at the age of five. There are men who like little girls and I'm sure you were a very pretty one. Can't you understand how terrible it has been for her not to *know*? To see you now, healthy and happy, will give her peace of mind."

I swallowed and looked at the ground. I had never tried to look at my situation from Maria's point of view. I hadn't wanted to. I had only been thinking of myself. I looked up into Leo's blue eyes and said in a low voice, "You're right. My mother in heaven must be ashamed of me. She would want me to be kind to this other mother."

The hand on my arm pulled me closer and I was enveloped in a warm, approving hug. I should have felt safe and comforted by his embrace, but the feel of his strong body against mine provoked a different sort of feeling. I wanted to put my arms around him and press even closer, I wanted....

Before I could do something stupid, an alarm went off in my brain and I backed away.

His arm dropped as soon as he felt me move. As I began to walk on, I said, "I will be nice to her. I promise. I will be nice."

"Good girl," he said. His voice sounded gruff and I wondered if I had insulted him by pulling away. The two of us turned onto the path that led to the back door of the house and finished our walk in silence.

*

It was Thursday and Elisabeth and I were comfortably ensconced in my sitting room when a knock came at the door. I put a finger in the page of the book I never tired of—*Ecole de Cavalerie* by Francois Robichon de Gueriniere. Elisabeth, who had been doing some sewing, put her work aside and went to answer the knock.

Leo stood in the doorway. He didn't come in, he only said, "I have come to tell Isabel that her mother is in the drawing room." He moved away from the doorway but left the door open.

Elisabeth came to stand beside my chair. She put her hand on my shoulder.

"You heard?" she asked softly.

"Oui."

"You must go, my love. Do you wish to change your dress?"

"Non." Lady Augusta had taken me into Lambourn to buy clothes to wear until I could go into London to shop in the expensive boutiques she had set her heart on. Today I was wearing a figured muslin day dress that was gathered under my breasts and fell to my ankles. I stood up, swallowed and said, "Pray for me, Elisabeth."

She put her arm around my shoulders and gave me a comforting hug. "You will make your *Maman* in heaven proud, Isabel. I know you will."

It was the right thing for her to say, and I straightened my back, lifted my chin, and marched to the door.

Leo was waiting in the hallway. "Would you like me to go with you or would you prefer to go alone?"

"I shall do this by myself," I said, and walked steadily from my sitting room down the hallway to the door that led into the big house then down that hallway to the drawing room. The door was open, and I inhaled deeply and walked in. There was a fire in the fireplace—it was a chilly day for June—and a small figure was standing in front of it looking toward the door. She was dressed in the exact shade of blue that was my favorite color. I stopped when I was about four feet in front of her and we looked at each other.

Her eyes were hazel, with fine wrinkles fanning out toward her hairline. Her hair was almost white. There were tears in her eyes, but she did not let them fall. "Charlotte," she said in a wavering voice. "Is it really you?"

"My name is Isabel," I said.

The tears fell.

My chest felt as if it was being squeezed in a vise. I made myself walk toward her. "There is no need to cry. I am fine. I have always been fine."

The sob she gave sounded as if it had been ripped from her soul. What I did next was pure instinct. I put my arms around her and said, "It's all right, I'm all right, there's no need to cry…" I kept repeating this as she wept her heart out in my arms.

She was a small woman with bird-like bones, and I patted her back as I would a child's. "I am sorry I caused you so much grief," I said.

Finally she stopped crying and stepped away from me, wiping her wet cheeks with a lacy handkerchief. "You must think me an idiot, weeping all over you like that."

"Not at all," I replied staunchly.

She gazed at me out of wet hazel eyes, and I realized that I had better take charge of this meeting or she was going to start crying again.

"Let us sit," I suggested. "We can talk better then, yes?"

She sat on the sofa I pointed to and I sat beside her. "Look," I said, pointing to the portrait that hung over the fireplace, "that is the reason Leo discovered me. It seems that I look very like his Great-*Grandmere*."

She turned her head to look up at the portrait. Then she looked back at me. "It's true. You could be twins."

"I know," I said, trying not to sound glum.

She made a little waving motion with her hand. "Will you tell me a little about yourself? About the family who...who..." She floundered looking for the right word.

"Adopted me," I finished.

"Yes." She sniffed. "Leo told me they were good people, that we were lucky that bloody nursemaid..." here her eyes flashed, "found them first."

"My *Maman* and Papa were the best people in the world," I said. "I love them with all my heart."

Her eyes closed. "Thank God," she whispered. "Thank God."

She looked so small sitting there in the corner of the sofa. I remembered Leo's words about how she had suffered, and I felt genuinely sorry for her. So I told her all about the Cirque Equestre and my life with horses. She hung on my every word, looking shocked sometimes, but still listening. I had just finished my recitation when Leo appeared in the doorway.

"May I join you?" he asked.

My mother said, "Leo, my dear, I can never thank you enough for finding Ch...Isabel for me. This is the happiest day of my life."

I could tell she really meant it, and felt guilty for not feeling the same way.

Leo came across the thick Persian rug and took the chair that sat at right angles to the sofa. He shot me a questioning look and I nodded to reassure him that I had indeed been a good girl.

We remained in the drawing room for another half hour until the gong rang, indicating it was time to dress for dinner. My mother and I were still sitting on the sofa and she turned to me and said, "You are an amazing girl, Isabel, and I am so thankful to have met you." Then she did something unexpected. She ran the back of her hand down my cheek in a gentle caress, and smiled at me.

That maternal gesture froze me and I stared into the hazel eyes that were fixed on me with such love. "My baby has grown into a beautiful young woman," she said tenderly, and suddenly I was overwhelmed by emotion.

This woman was my *mother*. Everything about me—my blood, my bones, my flesh—she had given me. She had carried me inside her for nine months and given birth to me in pain and suffering. I was part of her, and she was part of me.

The sob started deep inside me. *"Ma mere,"* I said. *"Ma mere."*

Small as she was, she gathered me to her, and I cried into her breast. I don't cry often, but when I do it's like a storm. I can't stop.

It was Leo's practical voice that finally got through to me. All he said was, "The dinner gong has sounded," but the calmness of his voice helped me to straighten up and wipe my cheeks.

"We must both scrub our faces well," my mother said humorously. "We don't want the rest of the family to know we have been crying over each other this whole time."

I managed a wobbly smile and nodded my agreement. Then the three of us left the drawing room and went up the stairs to change for dinner.

Chapter Ten

The following morning, I took my mother to meet Alonzo, and he surprised me by the way he responded to her. Alonzo is a very well-mannered horse. He graciously allows other people to admire him, he allows them to pat his neck and tell him how beautiful he is, but he is only affectionate with me. However, when Mother stroked his neck and told him how beautiful he was, he turned and looked down at her. His nostrils dilated and he pushed his head gently into her chest. She murmured some more. He lifted his head and looked at me, then back at her.

"We must have similar smells," Mother said. She was smiling but she had tears in her eyes.

Leo, who had been standing in front of the stable talking to Stoddard, came over. "Saddle up and show your mother just how wonderful he is."

So Alonzo and I put on a show just for my mother and she was awed. I listened to her express her wonder and appreciation of what she had just seen, and my heart swelled with gratitude. While my mother patted Alonzo and told him what a brilliant horse he was, I looked up at the sky and sent up a message.

You will always be first in my heart, Maman. *You saved me and loved me and taught me how I should live my life. I carry you with me wherever I go. You were the most unselfish person in the world, and I know you don't begrudge my happiness at finding this new mother. You will always be my* Maman.

As I stood there in the bright English sun, I felt peace envelop me. I had *Maman's* blessing. I felt it inside me, warm like the sunlight. I heaved a great sigh of happiness and relief and turned back to my horse and my mother.

*

The three of us had a light luncheon after which Leo asked us to accompany him to the library. He had something he wanted to discuss.

I gave a quick look at Mother and noted her grave face. Leo was grave as well. I had a flash of intuition and wondered if he was going to discuss the money that had been left to me. I had been trying not to mention the subject, thinking I should wait for Leo to bring it up.

Two chairs waited for us in front of the library desk. After Mother and I were seated, Leo took his own large leather chair behind the desk. An open folder with papers was already in place. He said, "I want to speak to you, Isabel, about the money that has been left to you. I waited for your mother to arrive because I wanted you to have some advice that wasn't all mine."

Mother looked surprised, then pleased. "That was thoughtful of you, Leo."

He nodded and their eyes met. He turned back to me and said, "As I previously told you, Henry is your half-brother, the only child of your father and his first wife. He was brought up knowing he would be the next Earl of Mansfield. His mother adored him and treated him as if he were a young princeling. Henry was furious when his father married again in hopes of having more children. He couldn't bear the thought of sharing his place in his father's affection. To be blunt, Isabel, he hated you. He hated the attention paid to the sweet little baby who had pushed him out of his place in the sun."

Leo paused and looked at Mother. "Would you say that was true, Aunt Maria?"

In a voice so soft it was barely audible she said, "Yes, Leo. Everything you have said is true."

Leo continued, "I am sorry to have to tell you this Isabel but when you were kidnapped, and the entire family was devastated, Henry seemed pleased."

Mother said sadly, "That is also true, Leo."

This brother sounded like a monster. "Why are you telling me this, Leo?" I asked. "I won't ever have to meet him, will I?"

Leo held up his hand. "I hope not, but I can't promise. He won't want you to get the money your father willed to you, and he'll do everything in his power to disprove your claim to be his lost sister." Leo's eyes held mine; he looked very serious. "The money is being held in a trust for you, but that trust ends when Henry turns thirty-five. At that time the one hundred thousand pounds will revert back to the estate. Henry has always assumed that money was his, but now that you are here it won't be."

A hundred thousand pounds! That was a huge fortune! "Was my father still hoping I would be found?" I asked Leo in an awed voice.

Leo and my mother exchanged a look then Leo said carefully, "I think he set up the trust because he didn't trust Henry's ability to manage money. Your brother likes the cards too much, and I think this was my uncle's way of keeping some of the family money out of his hands, at least for a while."

I looked down at my tightly clasped hands and swallowed. Without raising my eyes I said, "So my father wasn't thinking of me when he created the trust?"

Leo sighed. "I'm afraid not, sweetheart."

My mother said quietly, "If he knew that one hundred thousand pounds was being taken out of the estate for you, Isabel, he would be horrified."

I raised my eyes and looked at her. She was very pale. I said, "He doesn't sound like a nice man. I'm glad I had my own Papa instead."

My mother smiled at me.

I turned back to Leo and asked the only question that really mattered to me, "When do I get this money?"

A look of amusement came across Leo's eyes and brows and he said, "In some ways you are very French, Isabel."

I was insulted. I lifted my chin and said haughtily, "Money is only unimportant to those who have plenty of it. To those of us who inhabit a lesser world, it is extremely important."

His amusement turned into a grin. "Yes, mademoiselle."

I was annoyed—annoyed that he had made fun of me and annoyed that he was amused. I looked away from him before I said something I might regret.

Mother said, "Isabel is within her rights to know about her own money, Leo. When will she get it?"

Thank you, Mother. I gave her a grateful smile.

Leo became serious. "We first must prove Isabel's identity to my uncle's solicitor, James Sinclair. I'm sure Henry will do whatever he can to deny her claim, but one look at the portrait of Beatrice, and Sinclair should be convinced. Once we have done that, it is just a matter of paperwork to end the trust."

"When can we meet this solicitor?" I demanded. Leo's brows drew together and he looked at my mother. I turned and found her regarding me anxiously. She said in her soft, gentle voice, "Do you need this money immediately, Isabel?"

I lifted my chin. "As Leo said earlier, I am French. I like to have my money in my own hands."

Leo said, "I hope you aren't planning to return to France with a hundred thousand pounds in your purse, Isabel. That much money needs to be invested. It has been invested, in fact, and it has done very well. It would be foolish to take it out of the investments that are adding to your bank account."

"Who is in charge of these investments?"

"Your father named the Earl of Camden to oversee the account, so first my father and then I have been investing it for you. You can't simply withdraw all that money and hide it under your mattress!"

His tone put my back up, but I had enough sense to see the sense of what he was saying. I crossed my arms over my chest, scowled at Leo but kept my mouth shut.

Mother said, "Do you have a plan for this money, my love?"

Why not tell them? The money is legally mine. Leo said it was. They can't stop me from spending it the way I want to.

I spoke to Mother and ignored Leo. "My Papa is getting old and I want the money for him. He has worked hard his whole life and he deserves to retire and spend time with his horses without worrying about money."

Tears came to Mother's eyes and she smiled at me. "You love your Papa very much."

My answer came quickly. "He is the best man in the world, and I love him with all my heart."

Leo said, "We can set up a fund that will give him a generous income for the rest of his life. But you won't need the whole amount of the trust to do that. There will be money for a handsome allowance for you—and for an extremely nice dowry as well."

"A *dot*?" I looked at him in surprise. "I have no plans to marry, Leo."

"Ever?"

I had thought about marriage of course. Every girl thinks about marriage. But I had never met a man I wanted to marry. I had never met a man like my Papa. If I met a man like him…a man who was kind to the very marrow of his bones, a man whom other men respected and looked up to because he was such a shining example of what a man should be, a man who loved horses and children and making people happy— then I might think of getting married.

I answered Leo's question with a shrug and said, "My standards are high."

My mother said, "Good for you, my love. Good for you."

"I can't quarrel with an answer like that," Leo said. "You will have enough money to live unmarried if you so choose, but you ought to get to know some young men and see if you can find someone who will meet those high standards."

I was immediately suspicious. "What do you mean?"

"Your cousin Susan is coming on a visit and we all hoped you would join her at some local parties and dances this spring."

"This is Aunt Augusta's idea," I said immediately.

"Yes, it is, and I think it's a good one. You have promised to remain here for six months and only one of those months has gone by." The golden eyebrows lifted. "I hope you are planning to honor that promise. I don't think your Papa would like his daughter to renege on her word of honor."

I glared at him. "Are you trying to blackmail me?"

"Of course not."

His blue eyes held mine and I was the first to look away. "Of course I mean to honor my word," I said stiffly.

He gave me his most beguiling smile. "Good girl," he said.

To my great annoyance I found myself smiling back.

Chapter Eleven

Mother's arrival and Leo's assurance that I would get my money reconciled me to the fact that I would have to remain in England for five more months. And life at Camden Hall had become less foreign as I grew accustomed to it. The echoing hugeness of the house and all its fabulous treasures were no longer alien territory to me. Although I still missed our cozy farmhouse in France.

Mother and I passed many happy hours chatting in my sitting room or walking through the famous Camden Hall gardens. She told me her father, my grandfather, had engaged a gardener with the odd name of Capability Brown to design them and Mr. Brown had created something that was truly lovely. Mother and I would walk together along enchanting serpentine paths that wound their way through beautiful thick woods. There was even a Grecian Temple, which I privately thought looked ridiculously out of place in the midst of the English countryside.

The weather continued to be beautiful. It rained overnight, and the days were sunny and warm. During our walks together Mother reminisced happily about what it had been like to grow up at Camden. I told her frankly that her childhood sounded boring to me, and she laughed and agreed that it wasn't as much fun as growing up in a circus.

Mother also took on the role of peacemaker between Aunt Augusta and me. Ever since I had arrived Aunt Augusta had been trying to turn me into an English lady, and I had been resisting. My clothing was one of Aunt Augusta's chief complaints. How was I going to attend a dance when I had no evening gown?

English ladies dressed for dinner in what looked to me like fancy ball gowns. Margaret had a selection of these that she wore to dinner every night and she looked stunning in them. But I had never worn a dress without sleeves, let alone a dress that was cut as low as Margaret's were. I also did not have the breasts Margaret had.

The day after Aunt Augusta's disparaging remarks about my wardrobe my mother took me into Lambourn to buy a ball gown and a few other more appropriate dresses for dinner. She picked out the ball dress first.

"I can't wear a dress like that," I said as I looked at the skimpy concoction the shop owner was holding up in front of me. "It would fall off my front."

Mother laughed. "The seamstress will alter it to fit you, Isabel, and you will look lovely."

I was dubious, but when the dresses were finally delivered and I tried on one of the sleeveless low-cut dinner dresses, I was pleasantly surprised. I looked down at my front and was surprised that my small breasts looked quite womanly.

"I feel half naked," I confessed as I regarded myself in the mirror.

Elisabeth tut-tutted and Mother laughed. "You look beautiful, my love." She turned to Elisabeth. "Her hair is lovely. You are very talented, Elisabeth."

Elisabeth glowed. She was still a pretty woman, with light brown hair and dark brown eyes. She was fifty-one, but she did not look her age.

One of my biggest concerns about coming to Camden Hall had been for Elisabeth. At home she was part of the family; she lived with us, ate with us, went to church with us. It was very different for her at Camden Hall and I worried about it.

She seemed to exist in some half-world, not a servant but not family either. Fortunately, she and Mrs. Adams got along well, and Elisabeth took her meals with the housekeeper in her apartment. She was even learning English. But it wasn't the same as it was at home. Elisabeth had been a rock for me when I desperately needed her, and I loved her very much.

I think Mother understood this because she left to go down to dinner leaving us alone.

"You look beautiful, Isabel," Elisabeth said. Her eyes shone with unshed tears.

I went to give her a hug. She took a step back, telling me not to crush my dress, but I hugged her anyway. *"Merci,* Lisa," I said. *"Je t'aime."*

She gave me a wobbly smile. *"Je t'aime aussi."*

"I know," I replied in French. "And I am so grateful for that love, Lisa. I have so much to thank you for." We both started to sniffle.

Elisabeth held up her hand saying, "Stop. You cannot go downstairs with tearstains on your face."

I nodded and inhaled deeply. She patted my bare shoulder and I turned and marched resolutely out the door.

*

I had almost reached the drawing room when I heard Aunt Augusta's voice saying my name. With no feeling of guilt whatsoever, I stopped to listen.

"The child knows *nothing* about good society, Maria. *Nothing.*"

I looked up and down the hall and found it empty. I stepped closer to the doorway the better to hear.

"Before you came, she would spend her entire day down at the stables. When I asked Leo what she was doing for all those hours, he told me she was training one of his mares. What nonsense. Leo is an excellent horseman. He doesn't need a slip of a girl to train his horse."

Mother said, "Leo has always loved his horses. I'm sure it's something he and Isabel have in common. They seem to get along very well."

Aunt Augusta snorted. "I wish he would find a woman who interested him half as much as his horses do. He needs to marry again!"

Mother sighed. "Is it still as bad as it was?"

"Nothing has changed. It's ridiculous. Many men have lost a wife and baby in childbirth and it hasn't stopped them from marrying again. But it's impossible to talk to Leo about it. Whenever I mention marriage he gets this frozen look on his face and walks away."

"He must have loved Catherine very much," Mother said.

"That's all very well, Maria, but he has a duty to get an heir! It's ridiculous for him to spend the rest of his life mourning her. She was a beautiful woman but she's dead!"

I heard Leo's voice down the hallway and walked into the drawing room with as much calm as I could muster.

At last I had found out the truth about Leo's marital status. I felt sorry for him, of course. It was a terrible thing to have a happy occasion turn so tragic. I didn't like thinking of Leo as being so deeply in love that he refused to accept any other woman as his wife. In fact, it annoyed me. For once I agreed with Aunt Augusta. He needed to put it behind him and marry again.

The women had moved away from the drawing room door. I waited a moment before entering the drawing room then I went to present myself to Aunt Augusta. She smiled with pleasure at my low-cut blue gown. She beckoned me closer and stared grimly at my arm. I had no idea what she was looking at. I always washed when I came back from the stable.

I recognized Leo's step as he left the black and white marble floor and came onto the drawing room rug. Aunt Augusta turned her head toward the door and said in an awful voice, "Come here, Camden, and look at this chit's arm."

I stared at my arm as well. It looked the way it always did. What was Aunt Augusta talking about?

Leo came up next to me and I breathed easier. Whatever Aunt Augusta had found wrong I knew he would be on my side.

"Look at this arm, Camden," she demanded. She never called him Camden unless she was annoyed with him.

Leo looked. "Very pretty," he said.

"She has muscles! The child has muscles in her arms!"

Leo's warm fingers slid around my upper arm. He squeezed gently. The feel of his fingers made a strange little shiver run though me.

"And a very impressive muscle it is, Aunt Augusta," he said agreeably. "You can't train a thousand-pound horse without acquiring a few muscles, you know."

"It is not ladylike to have muscles." For some reason, Aunt Augusta was furious with him. I was growing extremely tired of Aunt Augusta.

"Isabel looks beautiful," he said. His hand was still on my arm and I still had that shivery feeling. He finally took his fingers away, saying, "A muscle only adds to the graceful curve of her upper arm. I think she looks quite lovely."

I gave him a grateful smile.

At this point, Robert and Margaret came into the room. Margaret stopped momentarily when she saw me then she came across the rug saying, "A gown. How lovely. Let me have a look at you Isabel."

I turned and prayed she wouldn't say anything about muscles. I had muscles in my back too. But Margaret was always correct; she smiled and told me I looked charming.

"Thank you," I said. She was wearing the deep burgundy gown that gave her pale skin the sheen of pearls. Even if I had the most gorgeous dress in the world I wouldn't look as beautiful as Margaret. Few women would.

I wondered if Leo's wife had been one of those few.

"Roger won't be joining us this evening," Leo said. I caught a note of disapproval in his voice.

"Where is that young scamp?" Lady Augusta asked, thankfully dropping the subject of my arm. In this house, when Leo spoke his mind the matter was settled.

Robert and Margaret and Leo were still standing, and Leo said, "Someplace he shouldn't be I suspect. Shall we go in?"

And so we did. Leo and Aunt Augusta, Mother and me, Robert and Margaret, all of us marching in a stately line to eat another overcooked meal.

Chapter Twelve

When I went down to the stable the following morning, I was surprised to see Robert and his two boys there ahead of me. David and Charlie had been home from school for a week, but I had seen little of them. They lived in the nursery on the fourth floor, and rarely made an appearance in the rooms we adults used. I once asked Margaret what they did with their day. She had treated me to a long green stare and said, "I keep them busy."

I smiled at both children and said hello. Each boy looked exactly like one of his parents. David had Robert's white-blond hair and blue eyes, and Charlie's coppery hair and green eyes made him a male replica of his mother.

"Can we see your horse, Isabel?" Charlie asked. "Uncle Leo says he's magnificent!"

"Of course you can see him," I said. "Let me ask Stoddard if he's still in his stall."

I collided into Leo when I turned into the stable doorway.

He grabbed my arms to steady me and I looked up into his concerned blue eyes. When I was close to him like this it always surprised me how big he was. "Are you all right, Isabel?"

"I'm fine. The boys want to see Alonzo and I was just going to check on him."

Two ponies were standing in the stable aisle. One was a sturdy-looking little fellow and the other an extremely fancy Welsh pony. Behind them grooms were tacking up Robert's bay gelding and Silver Boy.

"Are you going out with Robert and the boys?" I tried to keep the hurt out of my voice. He hadn't asked me to join them.

"Yes, we're going to ride out to Smithson's farm. The family have asked Rob for a new roof and he wants to get a closer look at the old one before he authorizes it."

I had joined Leo on several of his visits to the tenant farms and it had become one of my favorite things to do. The cozy farmhouses were a happy reminder of my home in France. I wondered why he hadn't included me in this morning's ride.

I tried to ignore my hurt feelings and asked, "Would you mind if I came along?"

"Of course I don't mind."

I was still smarting from not being asked to join them earlier and said a little sulkily, "You don't have to include me if you don't want to."

He looked surprised. "Of course I want you to come along. Rob and I sat up late talking and you had already gone to bed when we decided to take the boys out. I asked one of the footmen to put a note under your door telling you to meet us. Didn't you get it?"

The sun came back out in my life. I counted on Leo to be there for me in this strange place. I shook my head. "I didn't see it."

He shrugged, his big shoulders moving easily under the fabric of his riding coat. "Get Martin to saddle Alonzo. We'll wait for you."

Martin had just finished topping up the water buckets in each stall and was happy to help me get Alonzo ready. When I led my horse out into the sunshine, everyone was already mounted. The boys admired Alonzo, but I could tell they were disappointed. "He's not very big," Charlie said at last.

"Andalusians usually aren't," I said.

"We'll get Isabel to show you how he performs," Leo promised. "Then you'll see how special he is."

The boys agreed politely, but looked dubious.

Leo kept a pony for each of the boys. Charlie's was old, quiet and amiable; a good ride for an eight-year-old. David had just been given the fancy Welsh pony, but David was ten and big for his age. Rob was riding his nice-looking bay and Leo was on Silver Boy. I put my foot in Alonzo's stirrup and swung into the saddle.

The boys looked at me in astonishment. "You ride like a boy, Cousin Isabel!" Charlie said.

Leo looked at me to see how I would answer. "Alonzo doesn't like sidesaddles," I told Charlie.

"My Mama rides sidesaddle," David said.

"Most ladies do," I agreed.

"Shall we move off?" Robert suggested. "Isabel, why don't you and Leo go first with David, and Charlie and I will follow.

We arranged ourselves in the formation Robert had suggested and walked to the farm road that wound throughout the immense Camden Hall property. David talked enthusiastically about his new pony and Leo and I listened as we let the horses continue to walk. Once we had reached a straight run of road Leo turned to look back at Robert and asked, "Shall we trot?"

"Yes," Robert responded, and all the horses moved forward.

It was a day of mixed sun and clouds and the sun came out as we began to trot. We had gone about a quarter of a mile when David asked, "Can we canter, Uncle Leo?"

"Let me check first with your father." Leo turned his head and called to his brother, "Is it all right if we canter?"

I had turned to look at Robert as well, wondering why Leo would need his brother's permission. David was clearly a good rider; he had his pony under control.

Robert didn't answer immediately, and as I looked at him I thought that if Leo was a child of the sun, Robert was a child of the moon. The sun turned his hair and brows to silver and his eyes looked almost translucent under the brightness of the sky. He looked at his youngest son and asked, "How about a short canter, Charlie?"

Charlie who looked comfortable on his small pony, replied, "A short one, Papa."

All of the horses lifted into a canter. It was a beautiful day and I could feel Alonzo's energy under me. I didn't want to outpace David's pony, so I collected him a little. David was riding between his father and me when suddenly his pony broke into a gallop. I heard Leo curse then he brought Silver Boy back to a trot and steered him until he was directly in front of Charlie's little pony. I heard Robert saying to his son, "You're fine, Charlie. Punch isn't going to run after Gawain."

Leo said, "See if you can stop that fool boy, Isabel."

I slid my right calf behind the stirrup leather and Alonzo picked up a canter. By now David was out of sight around a turn in the road and I asked Alonzo for an extended canter. His long strides ate up the ground. We made the turn and I saw David ahead of me. His pony was still galloping. I wasn't sure which one of the pair ahead of me was in control, David or the pony, so I asked Alonzo for more speed. When we were close enough, I called, "David, slow that pony down!"

No answer and the pony continued to gallop. Alonzo and I overtook them, and I yelled that I was going to pass. We went by and I planted Alonzo's magnificently muscled rear in front of the pony and began to slow down. We moved from gallop to canter to trot to walk to a halt and I turned to look at David. He looked a little defiant.

"Are you all right, David?"

"Yes, Cousin Isabel." His voice was steady.

At this point Leo came riding up to us. "What were you thinking?" he said to his nephew. "And don't try to make me think that pony ran away with you. You're too good a rider to let that happen. You deliberately asked him to gallop."

"He wanted to gallop, Uncle Leo! He was bored. We were going too slow."

"I don't think it was Gawain that was bored, David."

No answer from David.

Leo said, "Before you took off did you think what would happen if Patches had followed you? He was right behind you on the path."

"Patches would never have left the rest of the horses."

"You don't know that. Charlie would have been terrified if his pony had started to gallop. You know how nervous he is since he took that nasty fall."

David hung his head and said, "I'm sorry, Uncle Leo. I didn't think of that."

"You are the oldest, David. You must always look after your brother."

"I know. I will. I promise, Uncle Leo. I would never want Charlie to be hurt."

By this time Robert and Charlie had caught up with us and Robert repeated much of what Leo had said. David apologized to Charlie and we continued our ride.

I thought Leo had handled the situation very well. He hadn't yelled at David or threatened to take away his pony, but he had made his point. Leo would make a very good father I thought and glanced at him out of the side of my eye.

*

After breakfast, my mother, Elisabeth and I decided to take a walk through the garden. The clouds had disappeared from the sky and the day was warm enough to wear a light dress. We spoke in French and Elisabeth and I told Mother some hair-raising stories of things that had gone wrong at the circus. Mother laughed until tears came to her eyes, and she kept saying how much she would have liked to be brought up in a circus.

When we reached home we met Leo in the front hall. He was dressed for driving. He gave us a distracted smile and said he was going to London for a few days. Some business had come up he had to attend to.

I tried not to show my dismay. He had virtually kidnapped me, and now he was deserting me? "How long is 'a few days'?" I asked. I heard my voice wobble and cleared my throat.

"I'll be back before Aunt Jane arrives with Susan." He smiled at Mother. "You'll be glad to see your sister, Aunt Maria."

Mother smiled back. "Yes, I will be. And John will be here at the end of the week as well."

John was Mother's husband, Sir John Hepburn, who lived in Scotland. When Mother wrote to him and said she wanted to spend a few more weeks at Camden Hall, he had replied that he would like to join us. Leo, of course, had immediately invited him.

Leo left, Mother and Elisabeth decided to take tea in my sitting room, and I decided I would go back to the stable and work with Gypsy.

Chapter Thirteen

Roger was down at the stable when I arrived. He smirked when he saw me and gave me that look—the one where he seemed to be undressing me with his eyes. I had once caught him trying to back Mary Ann against the wall to kiss her and I had warned him if I found out he was bothering the maids I would tell Leo. He had given me an unpleasant smile and *that look* but he went away. I told Mary Ann to come to me if she had any more trouble with him.

She gave me a grateful smile. "He's always been a nuisance, but he's getting worse. He caught Nancy dusting in the library the other day and scared her to death. She's new, a country lass, and she doesn't know how to handle a lad like Mr. Lavery."

"She should put her knee in his groin," I said bluntly. It was what Papa had told me to do in such a situation. I had never had occasion to use the maneuver, but I always remembered his advice.

Mary Ann's eyes opened wide and she stared at me in amazement. "That's what I told her," she said.

I nodded. "Good. And I meant what I said. Lord Camden would put a stop to Roger's activities if he knew."

Mary Ann gave me a grateful smile and we parted ways.

I was the second person to arrive in the drawing room before dinner that evening. The first person was Roger. I almost didn't go into the room when I saw him, but I was determined I wouldn't let him dictate my actions.

He didn't hear me at first. The rug was so thick that steps were muffled, and he was standing looking into the fireplace. I said, "Good evening, Roger," and he turned to look at me.

"Ah, it's the Circus Girl," he said. He gave me a nasty smile. "If you're looking for Leo he's not here. He's gone to London to visit his mistress."

I looked at him in bewilderment. "What?"

"Oh, no one has told you I see. I suppose they thought it wasn't fit for your *supposedly* virgin ears." He looked at me pityingly. "Leo keeps a little *pied a terre* in London where he has installed an actress named Helen Archer, whom he visits regularly to relieve his...er...manly needs. She's a beauty and she must know how to satisfy him because he's kept her for almost four years now."

My mouth dropped open. My heart was hammering, and a flush of blood had risen to my face. I didn't know what to say.

A pleased expression crossed Roger's foxlike face. "Sorry to spoil your plans to catch him as a husband, Isabel, but he has settled into permanent mourning for his lost wife. Robert is his heir and after Robert there is David. Leo apparently feels no need to produce a son of his own."

At this point Margaret came into the room, followed by Robert. Robert took one look at my face and said to Roger, "I hope you haven't been bothering Isabel. Leo told you he wouldn't stand for any nonsense from you."

This time it was Roger who flushed. "We've just been chatting." He looked at me. "Haven't we, Isabel?"

There was no way I was going to tell Robert what Roger had just said. It might not even be true. I forced a smile and agreed. My mother and Aunt Augusta came in and we all went in to dinner.

That night, alone in my bed, I thought about Roger's words. I was not an insipid little English girl. I knew that men had needs. The women who lived with the men in our circus were not always their wives. But Leo....

I was stunned. I was hurt. I felt betrayed. He was not the man I had thought him to be.

I told myself it was stupid of me to feel this way. I had no claim on Leo. I did not *want* to have a claim on Leo. I was looking forward to the end of my six months captivity so I could say goodbye to him and return to France and Papa.

I punched my pillow the way I would like to punch Roger's face. He was trying to poison my friendship with Leo, and I wouldn't let him do that. Leo and the horses were what kept me sane in this house. And my mother, of course. I focused my mind on my mother. Her husband was coming to stay with us for a few weeks, invited by Leo.

I had come to realize that Leo loved having his family around him. He was a man who should have many children. It was really idiotic of him to refuse to wed again...he must have loved his wife very much.

I jerked my thoughts away from Leo and concentrated on the other two family members who would be coming to Camden Hall shortly: Aunt Jane and my cousin Susan. Aunt Augusta had made plans for Susan and I to attend some local dances. I hadn't argued; I liked to dance and had thoroughly enjoyed the village dances back home. And Leo had promised he would teach me the English dances I would be likely to encounter.

I was back to Leo and once more I punched my pillow.

*

Two days later Susan and Aunt Jane descended on us with a carriage full of baggage. Aunt Jane was the youngest of Leo's aunts. She was a pretty woman with the family's signature blonde hair and blue eyes. Susan resembled her mother, and when we were introduced she gave me a happy smile and said, "I am so pleased to meet you, Isabel. Thank you for inviting me."

Leo had invited her, not me, but I simply smiled and said, "I'm happy you're here."

Aunt Augusta explained about Leo's absence and assured Aunt Jane he would be home the following day.

I felt a flare of happiness at this news, which was really a flare of relief that life would go on normally. Everyone—the servants as well as the family—had felt the absence of the master of the house. There was something about that tall golden presence that was immensely reassuring; one felt all was right with the world when Leo was near.

Susan and I decided to go for a walk in the garden before dinner so we could get better acquainted. Susan began the conversation as soon as we were out of earshot of the house by demanding, "Tell me about Leo!"

I had not expected this. "What do you want me to tell you?" I asked cautiously.

"Everything!" she said dramatically

I certainly wasn't going to tell her that he was in London visiting his mistress, so I didn't say anything.

"Start with how he found you," Susan suggested.

I was certain she must have heard the story from her mother, but I obliged, using a carefully neutral voice. I finished my tale by saying, "The facts made it impossible to deny that I was the missing child."

"It's like a novel," Susan breathed. We had reached one of the stone benches that were scattered along the garden walks and she took my arm. "Let's sit down."

I almost shook her off, but then gave in and joined her. A large planting of magnificent white flowers, whose names I did not know, stood on the opposite side of the walk. I stared at the beautiful blooms and said flatly, "It's not a novel; it's my life. I was perfectly happy as I was. I wish to God Leo had never seen me."

There was a small silence, then Susan reached over and put her soft smooth hand over mine. "I'm sorry I said that, Isabel. I've been so taken by the romance of your story that I never thought you might look at it differently."

There was genuine sympathy in her blue eyes and my heart softened. I said, "I promised Leo I would stay for six months, and I will honor that promise. But when the six months are up, I am going back to France and the circus and my papa. In the meanwhile, if Leo and Aunt Augusta want me to go to some dances and meet 'the right people' I will do it. But when my time is up, I'm going home."

Susan sighed. "It must be nice to have control of your own destiny. English girls must do as their parents wish." She looked at me with big eyes. "It must be great fun to belong to a circus."

"It is."

"Tell me about it."

The more stories I recounted, the bigger Susan's eyes got. "You are so lucky!" she said when I finally ended. "You must introduce me to Alonzo. And I want to see you ride!"

Susan certainly didn't seem as stiff and formal as I thought she would be. We continued our walk around the garden and she told me about herself. "I was supposed to have my Season last year, but my uncle died and we went into mourning. Mama said she wants me to go to some dances in the country before we go to London. That's supposedly her reason for coming to Camden."

"Supposedly?" I raised my eyebrows.

Susan glanced around, but there was no one within miles of us. She lowered her voice anyway. "Mama really wants to check on Leo."

"Check on Leo?" I was becoming an echo, but Susan was being decidedly enigmatic.

Susan stopped walking. I stopped as well. She took a step closer to me and said, "What do you think of him, Isabel?"

"What do I think of Leo?"

"Yes. Of Leo."

"Except for making me come here, he's been nice to me." I couldn't think of anything else to say.

"Leo is always nice," Susan said. Clearly she had not been satisfied with my answer. "My mother calls him the 'golden boy.' Everyone loves Leo. He could probably be Prime Minister if he wanted."

I made a noise of encouragement for her to go on.

Susan obliged. "To be fair, he did have a great tragedy happen to him. Have you heard about his wife and baby?"

Suddenly I felt uncomfortable. "I've heard," I said crisply.

"Mama and all the aunts think he is shirking his duty by not marrying. I think it's romantic, the way he clings to the memory of his first wife. They should leave him alone."

"I imagine he doesn't pay any attention to them."

Susan grinned. "I see you *have* got to know Leo. Mama complains about him all the time. She says it's his duty to pass on his bloodline, that he is selfish not to marry again."

"It's not as if he has no heir," I said. "Robert would inherit if Leo died, would he not?"

"Yes, he would. And Robert would make a good earl. He knows Camden Hall as well as Leo. And he has sons. But here's the rub. Robert isn't Leo. He will never be Leo." She inhaled deeply. "There is just something about Leo—and it's not only how he looks. When you're in his company you feel it..." Her voice trailed off and she shrugged. "It's hard to describe."

I understood what she was saying but I wasn't going to admit it.

"One can't help but love him," Susan went on. "Everyone in the family does. He's so kind. He's let Aunt Augusta live here forever even though she's unbearable, and he let Aunt Maria stay at the hall until she married again. He's taken in a whole series of cousins who needed help. Look at that swine Roger, living off Leo because he has gambled away all his money. He's also paying for Robert's boys to go to Eton."

"He's a good aristocrat," I said. "I don't usually approve of aristocrats. I think they should be done away with and their money given to the poor. But if England must have aristocrats, I will admit that Leo is a good one."

Susan stopped walking. "Do you mean that? About aristocrats?" she asked.

I stopped as well. "I do. The aristocrats in France lost their heads because of their greed. They took everything and ignored those who had nothing. They got what they deserved."

Susan was looking stunned. "Have you told this to Leo?"

"I have."

Susan wet her lips with her tongue. "Leo is a Whig. They are the progressive party here in England, but I don't think they're as progressive as you are."

"I doubt they want to do away with themselves," I agreed. I glanced at the sky and said, "We need to change for dinner, Susan. It's getting late."

The two of us walked back to the house in mutually reflective silence.

Chapter Fourteen

Margaret and I were both late to breakfast the following morning and we found ourselves in the awkward position of being the only two people in the dining room. This had never happened before, and I found myself hoping this might be a chance for us to become friendlier.

Margaret filled her plate and I made a point of sitting directly across from her at the table. She glanced up from her eggs and a faint line appeared between her perfect brows when her eyes met mine. I have found that sometimes it is best to be blunt and so I asked, "Why do you dislike me, Margaret?"

The line between her brows deepened. "Why should you think I dislike you?"

"You avoid speaking to me. Actually you avoid me altogether. Have I said or done anything to offend you? Please let me know if that is the case and I will apologize."

"You're being ridiculous." She put down her fork, took a sip of tea and regarded me over the rim of the cup. It was her usual hard green stare.

"You don't give that look to anyone else in the house," I said mildly, and took a sip of coffee.

"I don't dislike you, Isabel," she said stiffly.

"But....?"

She gave an annoyed shrug. "If you insist on having an answer, perhaps I resent you a little. Which is unfair, I admit, and I'm sorry I was so obvious"

"Resent me? But what have I done?"

"You haven't done anything." She shrugged again, still annoyed. "It's just that I can't help but compare the way you were welcomed into this family and the way I was welcomed."

She took another sip of tea. I nodded encouragement for her to continue.

She sighed. "Robert's family didn't want him to marry me. My father is the pastor of St. Michael Church in Lynnbury, a village near Lambourn. His father was the pastor there, as was his grandfather. My birth is decent enough." Her lips thinned and a bleak expression passed over her face. "However, my family has no money, and all of Robert's family wanted him to marry a girl with money. But Robert loved me and I loved him and Leo supported us."

I gathered from the way she said the last name that Leo's support had been the deciding factor in their courtship.

Margaret was going on, "So we married and came to live at Camden Hall. Robert has been Leo's steward ever since Leo came into the earldom and Leo wanted us to live at Camden. Robert wanted to keep living at Camden. Since I had no alternative to offer, we came to live at Camden. Leo gave us a big suite of rooms for our private use, and when the children were born we had the use of the nursery."

I thought about what I had just heard. "Surely you don't feel the family disapproves of you still?"

Margaret raised her perfectly arched eyebrows. "Aunt Augusta is Robert's godmother and she has never forgot that he married 'beneath himself.' And she never lets *me* forget that I am not worthy of the House of Camden."

I hadn't noticed any disapproval of Margaret from Aunt Augusta, but perhaps that was because she now had another focus for her displeasure. "She criticizes everything I say and do," I said gloomily.

"She has no idea how much I contribute to this household," Margaret said passionately. "*I* am the one who keeps all the household accounts. Robert cannot be burdened with ordering food for the table, or candles for the family and the servants, or hiring maids or new kitchen workers. He doesn't purchase new uniforms for the servants when they are needed. He doesn't meet regularly with the cook, the housekeeper and the butler. I earn my keep!"

Her beautiful skin was flushed, and her eyes were blazing green fire. I had the brief thought that I wouldn't want to get in Margaret's line of fire when she was in this mood.

I said, "Leo never treats you as a poor relation."

"Of course not. Leo is always perfect. I can have no complaint to make about Leo."

There was the slightest trace of acid in her voice. I deduced that Aunt Augusta wasn't the only one who had no idea about the amount of work Margaret did to keep the house running.

I said, "I'm so sorry, Margaret. I can understand why you might feel bitter about my arrival. Leo introduces me—a perfect stranger—into your midst and Aunt Augusta is thrilled to see me. My mother comes and is thrilled to see me. It isn't fair."

Margaret didn't answer but began to eat her breakfast. I felt I had said all I could say so I also began to eat. When I had finished my second muffin and was about to stand up, she said, "I'm sorry if I have been unfriendly to you, Isabel. My situation is not your fault."

I said conversationally, "If Aunt Augusta had lived in France she would have had her head cut off."

Margaret exploded into laughter. When she had composed herself again she said, "An opportunity missed."

We grinned at each other and I left the room.

*

Leo was home by teatime. This is an English custom where family and guests gather in the drawing room during late afternoon to drink tea. I was learning to like tea (although I will always prefer coffee) but the cakes and scones were wonderful. Someone in Leo's kitchen knew how to bake— probably a Frenchman. All of the family was present except for Roger and Margaret.

Aunt Augusta sat on a sofa behind the massive silver tea service, the chatelaine of the house dispensing comfort to the rest of us. I thought for the first time, *Shouldn't Margaret be doing this?*

I glanced toward Robert, who was sitting next to Susan on an elegant gold brocade sofa. He was saying something that made her laugh. He had made an excuse for Margaret today, and I suddenly realized that Margaret rarely came to tea; she was always 'engaged elsewhere.' I remembered our conversation of the morning and realized she might find it difficult to watch Aunt Augusta reigning in a place that should be hers. If anyone was the 'chatelaine' of this house, it was Margaret.

I was eating a scone from the little plate I had balanced on my knee when I felt a change in the atmosphere. I looked at the doorway, and there he was—the sun child himself. He smiled and advanced into the room going first to Aunt Augusta to kiss her hand then to Aunt Jane and Susan. He kissed both of them on the cheek and begged his aunt's pardon for not being there to welcome her and her daughter. The two of them glowed in his reflected light.

He hadn't even looked at me before Aunt Augusta said, "I hope you don't intend to join us with all the dirt of the road still on you, Camden."

The nerve of her, I thought. *This is Leo's house, not hers.*

Leo gave her his most beguiling smile. "I am very hungry, Aunt. If I promise to keep my dirt to myself may I stay?"

Of course she smiled back. "I spoil you," she said playfully, and handed him a cup of tea.

He took his cup and a plate of fairy cakes and finally looked my way. I had been late and was seated alone on a small French sofa. He began to cross the floor in my direction.

I watched as he approached me, effortlessly balancing his teacup and cake plate. He is truly an aristocrat, I thought. That beautiful ease is born from always having absolute certainty of oneself and one's position in the world. I knew I should totally disapprove of him. And I didn't. Now why was that?

He stopped, looked at the plate in my lap and said, "It looks as you've taken all the scones."

He sat beside me and I said, "Have one." He removed a scone from my plate and took a bite.

The conversation picked up where it had left off. The dance Susan and I would be attending was at the assembly rooms in Marlton, the market town closest to Camden Hall and the one where the estate did most of its local business. Robert sat on Marlton's town committee along with the local squire, pastor, and gentlemen of the more established local families. It was the perfect place for us to attend an assembly room dance.

The "genteel" and "presentable" young men we would meet sounded like dead bores to me, but I smiled and agreed. My plan for this English visit was the same as always—agree to everything until my six months was over, then collect my money and go home.

Aunt Augusta concluded her remarks that Leo had interrupted. "I am sorry I cannot attend myself, but Leo knows what a torture it is for me to sit in a moving carriage."

These words cheered me enormously. I had expected the old harridan to be there watching me like a hawk. I knew she had lumbago, but if it was keeping her from monitoring me at the dance it must be more serious than I realized. I felt a twinge of guilt that I hadn't taken her pain seriously.

Leo asked Aunt Jane about her husband and then he asked Susan if she would be going to London for the remainder of the Season.

"I hope so," she answered, glancing at her mother. "That is our plan at the moment."

"I have to find a house to rent," Aunt Jane explained. "We have been forced to miss the opening of the Season because of our mourning period, and it seems as if all the decently priced houses have been taken. I can't possibly launch Susan from a house outside Mayfair. It would look as if I were skimping on money."

"But you are skimping on money, Mother," Susan said. "You keep telling me how important it is to keep expenses down."

Aunt Jane flushed and Leo said to her, "Stay in Sommer House for the rest of the Season. It has a big ballroom that hasn't been used in years. Throw a ball to introduce Susan to society. She'll make a splash if you do that, Aunt Jane."

Susan's face lit like a candle. Silence from Aunt Jane.

"There's plenty of room for us all in the house if I should want to come to London myself," Leo said, sensing Aunt Jane's resistance. "Please don't concern yourself with that."

Susan, hands clasped to her breast, said, "Oh Leo, thank you!"

Aunt Jane said, "Leo, I have no plans to hold a ball for Susan. It would be too great a cost. But I thank you for your generous offer. I will find something I'm sure."

Leo stole another scone off my plate. "I'll cover the costs of Susan's come-out." He took a bite of my last scone. "It will be my pleasure. She's a great girl."

Susan grabbed her mother's arm and looked pleadingly into her face.

Aunt Jane went from being slightly flushed to being bright red.

I knew from Aunt Augusta that Aunt Jane had married a man who was beneath her own status as the daughter of an earl. Sir Henry Repton was a mere baronet and the local squire of his parish in Circencester. Baronets' daughters did not have titles, so Susan was simply Miss Susan Repton.

Aunt Augusta's nose was quivering, never a good sign. She said, in the voice she uses when she thinks she is getting the last word, "That is very generous of you, Camden, but I'm sure Sir Henry would rather provide for his daughter."

"Nonsense," Leo replied amiably. "Alex will probably say that I have more money than I know what to do with and I might as well spend some of it on his family."

Susan giggled and Aunt Jane tried to smother a smile. Both reactions told me that Leo had hit on the exact words that Sir

Alexander Repton would likely say when his wife told him about Leo's offer.

By the time tea was finished it was all but settled that Aunt Jane and Susan would occupy Leo's magnificent London mansion so Susan could make her debut.

Chapter Fifteen

The upcoming Marlton ball was the topic of conversation at dinner a few days later. It was not a topic that interested me greatly, but it was better than the overcooked lamb on my plate, so I paid attention. A problem had come up; Roger wished to come with us, and Leo did not want him to.

"What the devil do you want with a bunch of local misses?" he asked. "The squire's daughter, the parson's daughter, the local farmers' daughters. They can have no interest for an experienced man like you."

I studiously refrained from looking at Margaret when Leo said the words 'the parson's daughter.'

Roger was being stubborn. "Isabel will be there," he said, giving me a look that just missed being a leer. "And my cousin Susan too." Susan was next to find herself the target of the objectionable look. She turned very red and Roger laughed.

I was usually polite to Roger when we were with the rest of the family, but I was annoyed that he had made Susan uncomfortable and spoke before Leo could reply. "We are going in the coach and there is no room for you, Roger."

"I'll go with Margaret and Robert."

Leo said dismissively, "Robert is taking the curricle. There is no room for you there either."

"Then I'll ride," Roger persisted.

"I will send word to the stable that you are not to be given a horse." Leo didn't even sound annoyed. He had spoken and that was the end of it.

It was Roger's turn to flush. "You can't treat me like a child, Leo."

Leo held his cousin's eyes. "This is my house and while you are living here you will do as I say." His voice was soft, but it made me shiver.

"Fine." Roger pushed his chair back and stood. "I think I'll go to the tavern in town for my dinner. At least I'm welcome there."

"Do as you choose," Leo returned.

After Roger had stalked out Aunt Augusta said, "I don't know why you allow him to live here, Leo. He is *bad ton.* He always has been, and he always will be."

"He's here because he has nowhere else to go," Leo said tiredly, too generous to point out that the same situation applied to his aunt. "Let's not discuss Roger at the dinner table, Aunt. It's too depressing."

Aunt Augusta agreed, and the subject turned to dancing, and so to me. Did I know how to dance? Of course I knew how to dance. We loved to dance in France. Did I know the sort of dances that were performed in English ballrooms? Of course I didn't. I had never been in an English ballroom.

Susan, Aunt Jane, Margaret and Robert all immediately volunteered to help teach me, and after dinner we retired to the music room, which boasted a pianoforte along with various other instruments. Mother offered to play for us, and Robert volunteered himself and Margaret to demonstrate the steps.

The minuet, originally a French dance, was slow and stately as well as easy and boring. As almost all balls opened and closed with a minuet, I needed to learn it. It was not very complicated, and I quickly realized that I just had to follow the lead of the people around me. The quadrille was much livelier. Mother told me it had evolved from country dancing, and country dancing was what I knew. The cotillion was also energetic and fun. It was supposed to be performed by four couples, but we had only three: Margaret and Robert, Mother and Aunt Jane, Susan and me, and Leo with an imaginary woman. Leo was so funny, bowing and gesturing to his imaginary partner, that he had us all laughing.

When we finished the last cotillion, and it was almost time for tea again, Susan said, "What about the waltz? Mama says they do the waltz all over England now, even at local assembly dances."

"I don't believe it," Aunt Augusta declared. "That dance came from Vienna!" She uttered the word *Vienna* as if it were a synonym of Hell. "I can't believe that decent English gentlemen let their unmarried daughters dance the waltz!"

"My dear aunt, they dance it at Almack's all the time," Aunt Jane said with amusement. "I made certain Susan learned it. Nothing could be more embarrassing to a young girl than to be asked to dance and to have to refuse because she doesn't know how."

"They dance it at Almack's?" Aunt Augusta's chin was quivering. "Are you quite certain, Jane?"

"Quite certain, Aunt."

"Why do you object to it, Aunt Augusta?" I asked curiously.

"Because the man holds his partner in his arms and they dance together. As one." She stood up from her chair and said, "If you young people will excuse me, I am going to my bed. I find I do not wish to behold such indecency in my own house."

We all watched as she walked out. I could tell from the way she held herself that her back was paining her. I surprised myself by finding something gallant in the way the old lady stuck by her standards.

Aunt Jane said, "Since when has the hall become Aunt Augusta's house? I thought it belonged to you, Leo."

"It's her home," Leo said. "It has always been her home and it will continue to be her home until she dies. That's what she means when she calls it 'her house.' She's lived here longer than I have."

How kind Leo is, I thought. *He's never treated her like a pensioner. He respects her rightful place in the family order. He allows her the dignity of belonging.*

I felt ashamed of always being so irritated with an old lady who lived with pain. Maman and Papa would be ashamed of me. I vowed to be more patient and understanding the next time Aunt Augusta corrected me.

Mother was now at the piano and Robert and Margaret were standing on the open floor. Both their right hands were clasped and held aloft. Margaret's hand was on Robert's shoulder and Robert's hand was on his wife's waist. They were standing close but not touching. Mother began to play.

I watched as the two of them circled the floor in time to the music. They were looking into each other's eyes, and one could see the love they shared shining there. It was lovely.

Margaret began to count out the three-step timing for me and I watched her feet carefully. When Mother stopped playing Margaret said, "Come and dance with Robert, Isabel. He's a better dancer than Leo."

Robert and I danced. He counted steps, and, after I stepped on his toes a few times, I began to get the rhythm. He twirled me around a corner, and I went with him. He looked down at me and laughed. "*Brava,* Isabel! You're a quick study."

Susan said, "She certainly is. It took me hours before I could follow without stepping all over my partner."

Leo stood up. "Come along, Susan. Let's you and I join them."

Susan jumped up, put her hand into Leo's and they joined us on the floor. Mother played for five more minutes and then ended with a flourish. We all looked at each other and laughed. Mother said practically, "I would suggest that either Robert or Leo ask Isabel to dance if there is a waltz. I don't know if she'll manage to keep her feet to herself in the crowd of a ballroom."

Dancing with Robert had been fine. He had held me lightly and steered me with confidence. I hoped very much he would be the one to waltz with me if the dance should be played. The thought of waltzing with Leo made me nervous.

*

The dance at the Marlton Assembly Rooms was not unlike dances I had attended in our village in France. The clothing of both men and women was more expensive than what was worn by the farmers at home, but everyone was in high spirits and the dance floor was crowded. When our party was first announced, the entire room fell silent and stared. I knew they stared because they were astonished to see such highborn aristocrats at their little dance, but they were also staring at me. Apparently everyone within a hundred miles of Camden House had heard of my "return."

As Susan and I stood beside our respective mothers waiting for someone to ask us to dance, Robert came up with two young men on either side of him. It transpired they were the two middle sons of a well-off gentleman farmer and they would like to dance with us. Susan and I smiled and graciously accepted.

After the ice had been broken, we danced every dance. It was fun. The young men were shy, and in trying to put them at their ease I lost my own shyness. I checked on Leo periodically, and he and Robert were always deep in conversation with one of the few older men who were in attendance. Margaret, easily the most beautiful woman in the room, had decided not to dance and spent most of the evening in conversation with a woman I later found out was her cousin.

There were no waltzes, thank God. Not that Leo would have asked me. I don't think he looked at me once the entire evening, which I thought was unfeeling of him. He was the one who wanted me to "meet people." He might have bothered to introduce me to some of the people with whom he was having such deep conversations.

Susan was even more popular than I, and she was tired by the time we got back into the carriage to return home. She fell asleep on Aunt Jane's shoulder, and Aunt Jane herself looked as if she was dozing. Leo and I might have been alone in the darkened carriage.

When he finally spoke it was to say, "I didn't want to tell you before the dance, but your brother is coming to visit tomorrow. He is refusing to believe you are his lost sister, and I want him to see for himself how identical you are to the portrait of our great-grandmother."

His voice sounded soft and intimate in the privacy of the enclosed coach. All I wanted at the moment was to cuddle up to him and fall asleep on his shoulder, as I often used to do with Papa on late drives home. When I realized I was leaning toward him, I straightened my spine in horror. Leo was not my father. I wasn't precisely sure how I felt about him, but I knew my feelings were not those of a daughter.

He had said something else about my brother and I had to ask him to repeat himself.

"He's coming tomorrow afternoon and, unfortunately, he'll be staying for a while. He wants to speak to the solicitor who drew up the trust papers leaving you the money, and we're more convenient to Lambourn than Mansfield is."

"He's going to try to grab the money for himself, isn't he?"

"He is. But I think we have enough evidence to prove you are who you say you are." It was dark in the carriage, but I felt him turn to look at me. "Your father may have to come to England, Isabel. His testimony could be vital."

"But…Papa can't leave the circus! He is the glue that holds it together."

Leo took my hand into his large, warm clasp. "We are speaking about a great deal of money, sweetheart. If you wish to claim it, you will have to do everything in your power to prove your identity."

"I want that money," I said fiercely.

"Then I'll make sure you get it."

I believed him.

He seemed to have forgot he was still holding my hand as he asked, "Have you made any plans for the money as yet?"

There was the faintest trace of amusement in his voice and I took back my hand. "I told you, I want it for Papa. That inheritance is the only reason I agreed to come to Camden Hall with you, Leo. Papa is getting older, and I want him to be able to retire with enough money to keep as many horses, and as many people to help him, as he wishes. I want my Papa to live a long, long time, and that money will help him do that."

Leo was silent as we were carried through the silent night together. We were almost home when he spoke again. "What sort of future do you see for yourself, Isabel? Don't you want to marry and have your own family? Surely it would be wise to keep some money aside for yourself. Even a quarter of what is in the trust is enough for you to make a very good marriage."

"I have never met a man I wanted to marry, and I don't want to marry someone I don't love."

"May I ask what are you looking for in a husband?"

The answer to this question was easy. "A good man. A kind man. A man who likes to laugh. A man who loves children. And, of course, he must love horses as well."

"In short, a man like your Papa."

I smiled up at him in the dark, pleased he had figured that out. "Yes. I want a man exactly like my Papa."

"Hard to find someone like that."

The picture of Leo allowing Aunt Augusta to call Camden Hall "her" house slipped into my mind. I shook my head to banish it. "Yes," I said. "It is."

Chapter Sixteen

Two more family members arrived at Camden Hall the following day. Mother's husband, Sir John Hepburn, arrived from Scotland in time for luncheon, and my brother, Henry, Earl of Mansfield, arrived from Surrey in time for tea.

Sir John was a bear of a man. When Mother stood beside him, she looked like a child. It soon became evident, however, that Sir John adored his wife, and his feeling seemed to be reciprocated. Mother looked radiant, and Sir John was warmly welcomed into our household.

My brother had a different kind of reception. We were at tea in the drawing room, even Margaret was present on this day, when Hobbs appeared in the doorway and intoned, "The Earl of Mansfield, my lord."

Every head turned toward the door and my brother walked in. The first thing I noticed was his hair. It was ink black and he wore it unfashionably long. Leo rose from his seat by Robert and approached him, hand held out. "I'm glad you could come, Mansfield. Welcome to Camden Hall. I believe you are acquainted with most of the family, but you must let me introduce you to your sister, Lady Isabel Lewins."

My brother strode across the room and stopped in front of the sofa where I was seated. I had put down my cup of tea as soon as he entered so I was able to extend my hand. Before I could speak a word of greeting, he snapped, "My sister? That is something that remains to be proved."

The narrowed eyes staring down at me were gray and hard as the rock on Lambourn Downs. I returned my hand to my lap, narrowed my own eyes and held his stare. For a long moment neither of us spoke but we both knew war had been declared.

Leo's voice broke our stalemate. He said, "Mansfield, permit me to show you the portrait of our great-grandmother that so resembles Isabel."

Henry swung around and took a few steps toward the wall where the infamous portrait was hanging. He looked for a few moments in silence then shrugged. "There is a certain resemblance; perhaps she does have some Sommer blood in her veins. But she could be the genetic copy of some by-blow your family never knew about. In fact, that's what she probably is. You will never be able to prove her identity legally."

Aunt Augusta said in a frigid voice, "Be seated, Mansfield, and do not speak of Isabel as if she were not present. It is very rude, and I do not permit rudeness in my house."

I thought of the times Aunt Augusta had been rude to me and my jaw dropped. Then I realized—she was defending me. My jaw snapped closed and my eyes widened.

Henry said, "I always thought this was Leo's house, Aunt Augusta."

Oh my God, I thought. *Twice in two days.*

But Aunt Augusta had a champion. His voice frigid, Leo said, "It is my house and Aunt Augusta is my hostess. And if you cannot keep a civil tongue in your head, Mansfield, you had better leave."

My brother shrugged and took a seat on one of the many empty gilt chairs. "Sorry, Lady Augusta. I didn't mean to insult you."

Hah! I thought.

Aunt Augusta said, in a voice that was as frigid as Leo's had been, "Will you take some tea?"

"I will."

Aunt Augusta poured. Henry remained where he was. Susan said breathlessly, "I'll take it to him, Aunt Augusta." She collected the teacup and saucer and brought it to my brother.

He thanked her, ran his eyes over her from head to toe and said, "And to whom do you belong, little girl?"

Susan's face flushed bright red and she hurried to resume her place.

"Susan is my daughter," Aunt Jane said, from where she was sitting on the sofa next to Margaret.

The arresting black head turned. "Ah, yes. Aunt Jane. The baby sister. You're looking well."

"You didn't bring your wife?" she asked.

"No. She has just lost a child. Not up to a long carriage ride."

"I am sorry to hear that," Aunt Jane said with genuine sympathy.

"So am I," Henry returned, his face grim. "She finally gets with child and then she loses it. And it would have been a boy. A most infuriating situation."

No one had anything to say to this comment. Henry lifted his teacup to his lips and looked at Leo. *If looks could kill*, I thought, and shivered. Leo made a general comment about the new curate at the rectory and everyone took up the new topic with relief.

*

Once tea broke up Susan and I went for a walk in the garden. I knew she was dying to discuss my brother, and I wasn't averse to such a prospect. As we walked among the bountiful beauty of Mr. Brown's creation, she used every derogative adjective she could think of to describe the Earl of Mansfield.

"He certainly sounds heartless," I agreed. "That was a terrible thing to say about his poor wife who had just lost a baby."

"That's the way he is. It's the way he's always been. If he wants something, he expects to get it. His poor wife hasn't managed to produce an heir yet and I can only imagine what her life must be like."

"He doesn't have any heir?"

"Well of course he has an heir. Estates like Mansfield are always tied up in an entail. If Mansfield doesn't have a son, the estate and title will go to some cousin."

"How can someone who has everything be so nasty and…and…I searched for the English word. *"Wicked,"* I finally said.

The sky overhead was blue, and a breeze was stirring the leaves on the trees. I thought it was a shame our peace should be disturbed by this snake of a brother.

Susan said, "He was an only child and Mama says his father adored him. He encouraged Henry to be proud of his ancestry and to look down on all lesser beings. To be just like the earl himself, in fact."

I bent to remove a twig from our path. "I'm so glad your parents discussed these kinds of family matters with you, Susan. You're my best source of information."

She glanced at me and grinned. "They don't discuss anything with me. I get everything I know from listening to the servants. They discuss everything all the time." I started to laugh, and she joined in. "I'd hardly know my own name if I had to rely on the information I got from my parents," she added.

We walked in comfortable silence for a while then, with some hesitation, I mentioned what had bothered me most about my brother's arrival. "What Henry said…about me being the child of a bastard…do you think that might be true, Susan?"

She stopped walking and I stopped as well. She turned to look at me, settling her shawl more snugly around her shoulders. The breeze was getting stronger.

"Of course it's not true! How could you even think that, Isabel?"

"It's not impossible, Susan. You must admit that."

"It may not be impossible, but it's certainly incredible. You were given away on the very same day Aunt Maria's baby was stolen from her pram. You were the same age as that baby. And you look exactly like a portrait of your great-grandmother. What are the chances that you were a different baby, also stolen, who happened to be the offspring of some bastard member of the Sommer family, who grew up to be the exact image of our famous great-grandmother?"

When put like that, it did seem incredible that I could be someone other than who Leo had said I was.

Susan said, "It's getting chilly, Isabel. We should go back to the house. It will soon be time to change for dinner."

When I was once again inside the walls of Camden Hall I first went to my sitting room. When I heard the voices of Elisabeth and my mother, I backed quietly away, returned to the stairs and went to my bedroom. I needed to be alone. I had something to think about.

When my brother said I might be the offspring of a bastard, my heart had jumped in surprise and I realized I had never doubted the truth of my new identity. I had fought against it, been angry about it, been determined to hate every second I spent at Camden Hall, been determined to hate Leo, but I had never doubted the truth of my identity.

And now…if the possibility of my not being Maria's daughter were true, shouldn't I have been thrilled? I should have been packing my bags to go back to Papa and the old life I missed so much. Instead, I had been appalled.

I sat in the comfortable red velvet chair in front of the fire, stared into the empty grate, and thought about this. It was true I had grown more comfortable here at Camden. It was true that Alonzo was happy here, and true also that I was enjoying working with Leo's horses. I liked spending time with Leo; he was good company. But Camden wasn't *home*. Home was the circus. Home was our beloved farmhouse. Home was Papa.

Papa!

Papa had been the reason I had been so appalled! If I weren't the girl Leo thought I was, then I wouldn't get the money for Papa.

The door opened suddenly and Elisabeth came in. "I am so sorry, Isabel," she said, coming to me and dropping a kiss on the top of my head. "Your *Maman* told me about that terrible man and the things he said. She told me a mother always knows her own child, and from the moment she first hugged you, she knew you were her daughter."

I was so relieved to hear this that I jumped out of my chair and hugged my dear friend. "Thank you for telling me that, Lisa."

She held me to her breast. *"Do not worry* mon ange. You are who the Earl of Camden has said you are. No one can take that away from you. The money for your *dot* will still be yours."

I thought of Leo's comment that the French always think of money first, and I almost smiled.

Chapter Seventeen

We sat down to dinner with two more men than we usually had. Mother's husband, Sir John, was lovely and entertaining. I cannot make the same comment about my brother. He spoke rarely, and when he did his voice was cold and sarcastic. I particularly resented the tone he took when he spoke to Aunt Augusta. She lived here. He didn't. He should show her some respect.

As usual, the family spent the evening in the drawing room. My mother played for us on the pianoforte and Margaret sang. Aunt Augusta had given up trying to get me to perform. I could sing, but not like Margaret. My only talent needed a horse as an accompaniment, not a piano.

Aunt Augusta always retired early, and tonight the rest of us followed. It had not been a lively gathering. As soon as they had swallowed their tea, Leo and Robert fled to the billiard room. Roger and my brother disappeared not long after, leaving Sir John Hepburn as the only man. Aunt Jane suggested we all retire early, and no one disagreed.

I wasn't at all tired, and when I was halfway up the stairs I decided to pay a quick visit to Alonzo. I waited inside my room until I was sure the others were safely into their rooms, told a disapproving Elisabeth I would be back shortly, returned down the stairs and made my way through the now familiar maze of corridors that ran through the old house. I reached the door I wanted just as Hobbs had finished locking it.

"I'm going to take a quick trip to the stable, Hobbs," I explained to the surprised butler. "Can you leave this door open until I get back? I won't be long."

"It's dark outside, my lady," he replied. "A little late to be out by yourself."

"The moon is out and I won't be long."

He hesitated and I repeated, "I'm only going to the stable. If you give me the keys, I can lock the door myself when I return."

He was horrified. "I cannot let you have the keys, my lady! I do not think my lord would approve."

By now I had become absolutely determined to see Alonzo. "Come back in half an hour, Hobbs. I will have returned by then and you can lock the door."

He did not look happy. "Allow me to summon one of the footmen to go with you, my lady."

"I do not need a footman. I am perfectly capable of walking to the stable, seeing my horse, and returning here within half an hour's time."

He still looked unhappy, but he gave in. "Very well, my lady. I will return in half an hour and lock the door."

"Thank you." I opened the door and let myself out.

The sky was clear, and the moon's silvery light showed me the way to the stable. I muttered to myself as I walked along the familiar path. Why did the English treat their young women as if they were children? Or imbeciles? In France, in the circus, I was respected as an adult.

I reached the stable in perfect safety. One of the large front double doors was open to allow the horses fresh air, and inside the stable a horse whinnied. I was about to go inside when I noticed a glove on the ground just outside the closed door. When I straightened from picking it up, Roger stepped through the stable's open door out into the moonlight.

"What are you doing here?" The two of us exclaimed at the same moment.

I answered first. "I have come to pay a visit to Alonzo. Why are you here?"

"I was planning to saddle a horse, but now I see there might be more fun right here than at the pub."

While we were speaking Roger had come over to me. His move left me facing him with my back a few steps away from the stable door. The moonlight showed me the look in his eyes, and I didn't like what I saw. I said, "You had better return to the house. I don't think Leo would approve of your taking out one of his horses this late at night."

"What Leo doesn't know won't hurt him." He stepped closer to me and I took an instinctive step away, which put my back right up against the heavy stable door. Roger followed, bracing his two hands against the door on either side of me, holding me prisoner. His face was close to mine and I could smell the brandy on his breath. "Everyone thinks you're a virgin, Circus Girl, but I know better."

"Get away from me!" I said furiously, and prepared to knee him where it would hurt.

He leaned his entire body against me, blocking my knee with his weight. "Oh no you don't." He was laughing. "I know that little trick."

All of a sudden I was frightened. Very frightened. "If you touch me, I'll tell Leo," I said.

His head was bent toward mine and I could feel his hot brandy-reeking breath on my face. "The Great God Leo," he muttered. "Can't wait to see his face when he learns I got in before he did." And he lowered his mouth to mine.

My head was pressed against the door and his mouth was grinding my lips into my tightly shut teeth. I struggled against him, but I was helpless against his superior strength. I tried to scream, but when I opened my mouth his tongue smothered my cry. I couldn't breathe. I couldn't get my knee up. I was powerless. I shut my eyes tightly and asked God to help me.

Then, all of a sudden Roger was gone. I opened my eyes, but I was shaking so badly I couldn't see. I blinked and the scene in front of me came into focus. Roger was lying on the ground and Leo was standing over him.

God had heard my prayer.

As I watched, Leo lifted Roger off the ground with one hand on his coat, and flung him away as if he were a sack of grain. "I want you gone by tomorrow morning," he said. "Pack whatever you own and get out."

Roger was cringing on the ground, blood dripping from his nose. "You can't throw me out, Leo," he whined, trying to wipe his nose. "I have nowhere to go."

A rush of satisfaction swept through me when I saw the blood. Leo had punched Roger in the face. I hoped his nose was broken.

"You have abused my hospitality by attacking a young girl who is under my protection. I cannot have you anywhere near Isabel. Do you understand me, Roger? I want you out of my house. Immediately."

Roger began to scramble to his feet. "But where can I go?" Now it was his turn to be frightened.

Good, I thought.

Leo said, "I don't give a damn where you go as long as it's far away from Isabel. I don't want to see or hear from you again."

"But I have no money!" By now Roger was on his feet and maintaining a safe distance from Leo.

There was a pause. Then Leo said in a calmer voice, "I'll leave some money with Hobbs. You may ride Brownie to the inn and I will collect him in the morning."

Leo's sense of responsibility was reasserting itself. Too bad, I thought. I would have liked to see Roger starve.

Roger was looking stunned as well as frightened. "But...she's only a circus girl, Leo. It's not as if she's a real lady."

I saw Leo's hands close into fists.

I said hurriedly, "Get out of here Roger before Leo kills you." I wouldn't mind seeing Roger dead, but I didn't want his blood on Leo's conscience.

Roger went.

*

After Roger disappeared into the stable Leo turned to me. "Are you all right, Isabel? Did he...hurt...you?"

"He scared me, Leo." My voice trembled. "I couldn't fight him off. If you hadn't come, he would have raped me."

"That's certainly what it looked like." Leo looked very white in the moonlight, very white and very angry. I knew this situation was partly my fault; I shouldn't have come out here alone. I said in a little voice, "I'm sorry."

He didn't answer and I started to shake again. If Leo hadn't come....

He said, "You're safe now, sweetheart."

He opened his arms and I went into them.

Oh the comfort of being in Leo's arms! He was much stronger than Roger, but I knew that his strength would always be used to protect me, never to harm me. I started to cry and then couldn't stop. I soaked the shoulder of his coat, and he rubbed my back and spoke softly into my ear.

When I had recovered myself somewhat, I lifted my tear-streaked face out of his shoulder and looked up at him.

The moonlight showed me the familiar chiseled bones of his face, but his blue eyes were dark and unreadable. I produced a wobbly smile and said in a wobbly voice, "Thank God you came."

Our bodies were still touching, and my face was turned up to his. He didn't answer; he just bent his head and kissed me.

My initial feeling was shock. What was Leo *doing*? But then something in me leaped in response and I slid my arms around his waist, leaned into him and kissed him back. His arms tightened. My heart was pounding. I could feel his kiss all the way down into my stomach. It was wonderful.

The spell was broken when his hands grasped my shoulders and lifted me away from him. We stood in the moonlight looking at each other and I knew that everything between us had changed.

"I should not have done that," he said. "I'm sorry Isabel."

Sorry? What did he mean? I looked up into his darkened eyes and hard-set face. "Why should you be sorry?"

"I took advantage of you; you were frightened and you turned to me for comfort. Christ! I'm almost as bad as that bloody Roger!"

"You are nothing like Roger. I hated Roger's kiss, but yours...I liked yours, Leo." I gripped my hands together to keep from reaching up and smoothing the hair that had fallen across his forehead. "I liked it very much."

He ran his hand through his hair, dislodging more golden strands. He didn't say anything, and he was starting to look grim.

I said, "If it was such a terrible thing to do, why did you do it?"

The grim look softened a little and he said, "I have been wanting to do it for a long time, Isabel. I'm afraid the events of the night caused me to lose my restraint."

I stared at him in astonishment. "You've wanted to kiss me? You never told me that!"

"Your father trusted you to my care. I have behaved abominably."

"Perhaps you should behave abominably again," I suggested. That kiss had been earth shattering.

"Don't tempt me."

The look on his face stopped me from saying anything else.

"You are going to come up to the house with me, and in the morning I will tell the others that Roger decided it was time for him to leave." He took my arm rather roughly and began to walk me up the pathway.

"How did you know to come and look for me?" I asked, as I skipped to keep up with his long steps.

"Hobbs told me you had gone to the stable by yourself. He was worried about you. He knows Roger and he knew Roger wasn't in the house."

I felt terrible. "I was rude to Hobbs and he was my savior. I will beg his pardon tomorrow."

"That would be most appropriate."

We had reached the doorway and before he could open it I put a restraining hand on his arm and said softly, "Leo...?"

He sighed. "I know. It's unreasonable to expect you to forget what happened. Tomorrow, after we both have had a chance to think, we'll talk."

"Shall we ride out early?"

"I'll meet you at the stable at seven."

"Good."

We were standing inside the doorway and Leo had the key in his hand. He said, "Go to bed, Isabel. I'll lock up here."

I wanted to touch him so badly, but I knew he didn't want me to. So I left him there and went upstairs to bed. I didn't fall asleep for a long time.

Chapter Eighteen

I lay awake for a long time. Something serious had happened between Leo and me tonight; so serious that I didn't think we would ever be able to return to what we had been.

I had never before thought about the nature of my friendship with Leo. We had ridden together, laughed together, talked about Camden Hall and what it meant to him, what his responsibilities were to his tenants and his family. I had talked about the circus and my life on the road. We had even talked about our revolution in France, and he had listened seriously when I explained it to him from the point of view of struggling French families. He had been my friend.

That kiss had changed everything. It had not been a kiss of friendship. It had not been a kiss of comfort. It had been a kiss of passion. And I liked it so much I had kissed him back.

What would he say when we rode out this morning? I didn't think he would simply apologize and ask me to forget it. He thought he had violated Papa's trust by kissing me. I took a deep shuddering breath as I realized what he probably would do.

He would ask me to marry him. For him it would be the honorable thing to do. The question for me was: how would I answer? Could I give up my life in France with Papa for a man I had known for only two months? Could I live in this suffocating society and be happy?

I thought again of last night's kiss and my heart knew I would respond like that only to Leo.

I flipped over on my back and stared at the ceiling. The bedroom windows were open and I could hear the sound of the breeze blowing through the tree outside my window. From somewhere close by a nightingale called.

I wouldn't mind living here at Camden Hall. It was a beautiful place and I had grown comfortable with this new family. My thoughts turned again to Leo and I began to enumerate what I knew about him.

He was a good man. That was the first thing that came into my mind. Leo was a good man. He was kind and generous. I knew he found Aunt Augusta trying, but he always treated her with respect. He had let Roger stay at Camden Hall even though he didn't like him. He had welcomed my mother and her husband and Susan and Aunt Jane into his house. He had offered Susan the use of his London house as soon as he heard of Aunt Jane's financial situation. He was the head of his family and he took his responsibility seriously. He had even given money to that *batard* Roger before he banished him.

He was a good steward of his inheritance. I had seen for myself how well his tenants lived and how easy they seemed to feel in his company. If the French aristocrats had behaved like Leo there would have been no need of a revolution.

He had always been kind to me. He had understood how alien Camden must seem to me, and he had done his best to make me comfortable and less lonely. He was a good man.

I drifted to sleep in the midst of these thoughts and awoke a few hours later. It was early morning; Mary Ann had not yet been in to start my fire. I dressed in my riding clothes and crept through the sleeping house to a window in the old house that was at ground level. I knew the latch was broken and it was easy to open the window and climb out onto the turf. Hobbs wouldn't be opening the back door for another hour. I had used the window occasionally in the past when I couldn't sleep and wanted to be with Alonzo.

It was a chilly morning and I was happy to let myself into the warmth of the stable. It was still too early for the horses to be fed, and they were all sleeping or resting quietly, confident their hay and grain would soon arrive. I walked down the aisle to Alonzo's stall and looked in. He was stretched out on his side, his legs sticking straight out, and he was snoring. I thought, as I had often thought before, that my horse had the best temperament of any horse in the world.

I called his name softly and he stirred. He saw me, heaved himself to his feet and came to the front of the stall to greet me. I had brought some carrots and he was pleased to eat them. When he had finished, I went into the stall and used the brush I had brought to groom him. I knew all of his itchy spots and he enjoyed the attention very much. When I finished I curled up in the corner, my back to the stall wall, my knees pulled up to my chest. Alonzo began to pick through the straw bedding, looking for pieces of last night's hay he might have missed.

Wherever we had been, the corner of Alonzo's stall had always been my refuge. When I was worried, or angry, or unhappy, I would retreat to that corner, watch my beloved horse do what he was doing just now, and feel peace and courage steal back into my heart.

Alonzo was happy here and that was important to me. He liked Stoddard—who also knew his itchy spots—and he liked the big grassy turnout pen he had to himself. He liked Gypsy. In fact, I was beginning to think he liked Gypsy too much. Although a foal with Gypsy's fineness and Alonzo's conformation…how beautiful would that be!

I heard voices at the door and stood up slowly. The horses had heard the voices too and they were all at the front of their stalls, nickering. They knew breakfast was coming.

I gave Alonzo a kiss on his soft muzzle, brushed myself off and slipped back into the aisle. I still had no idea of what I was going to say to Leo.

*

Leo arrived half an hour later and Matthew, one of the younger grooms, saddled Silver Boy for him while Stoddard himself saddled Alonzo. Stoddard had fallen in love with Alonzo. The first time he had seen Alonzo work he had greeted me with tears in his eyes. He was a man who knew and loved horses and he treated Alonzo as if he were a prince. Which he was.

The morning chill was fading from the air as Leo and I rode out of the stableyard. As we approached the bridle path, I thought back to the first ride we had taken together. I had been on Alonzo and he on Silver Boy, and we had hardly known each other.

We didn't speak as we cantered side by side along the path that would take us to the spot by the river where we liked to stop. The sun's morning rays were strong enough now to reflect off the surface of the swiftly moving river, and we left the horses to graze while we took our usual spot on the sandy ground near the river's edge.

I sat and Leo lowered himself to sit beside me. The ground was a little damp and he asked, "Is it dry enough for you?"

"It's fine."

He was looking at me, but I kept my eyes on the river. I had the strange quivery feeling in my woman's parts I had felt last night and it made me nervous.

I heard him let out a long breath, then he said in a deeper voice than usual, "You must believe me when I tell you this, Isabel. The only reason I insisted that you come to Camden

Hall was for the sake of your mother. I knew you were unhappy here, and I tried to spend time with you because I was the cause of your unhappiness. But the better I knew you, the more I liked you, and...well, I'm afraid I have ended by falling in love with you, sweetheart. Do you think you could try to love me back? I very much want to marry you, you see."

I took a quick look at him, then looked away again. The morning sun was shining on his hair and the eyes looking at me were bluer than the sky. He was perfectly still, making no motion to approach me. There was such beautiful serenity about Leo, I thought. It was one of the things that had first drawn me to him.

I thought about last night again and swallowed hard. "Leo, I love you too, but I don't know if I can marry you. I don't know if I can leave Papa."

"Isabel," he began.

I shook my head, fixed my eyes on the rushing water of the little river, and continued bravely, "I don't know if I can marry a man who will always be comparing me to the wife he lost."

He didn't answer, and when I gathered the nerve to turn my head, he was looking grim. "Who suggested such a thing to you?"

I ignored his question and posed one of my own. "Is it true? Are you still in love with your wife? I need to know the truth, Leo. If I am to give up the only life I have ever known, I need to know the truth."

"The truth." His voice was grim. "I have never told anyone the truth."

All of that perfect serenity was gone; I had killed it with my words about his wife. But I wouldn't give up. "I need you to tell me, Leo. If I decide to be your wife, I need to know."

He got to his feet, went to the edge of the river and stared into the rushing water. I watched his rigid back and said nothing.

Finally he turned to face me. "All right, I'll tell you. But it's not a pretty story, Isabel."

I held his eyes, which had turned so dark they looked almost black, and nodded encouragement.

He remained standing by the river, maintaining the distance between us. "I was twenty years old when I married Lady Catherine Lambert. She was eighteen, the only daughter of a wealthy viscount and she had a dowry my father was anxious to acquire. Her father owned a large piece of property in Kent, adjacent to a property owned by my family. The viscount's property would more than double our property's size, and my father had plans to build a splendid new house there. The Kent location would be much closer to London and my father was active in Parliament."

He paused. His face was expressionless, but his eyes were almost black. "I had no say in the matter. I was my father's heir and I was expected to agree to his choice of a suitable wife. And when I met Catherine I was dazzled. She was the most beautiful girl I had ever seen. She had thick black hair and long curling eyelashes. Her eyes were green and her mouth was pink. I thought I was the luckiest man in the world and couldn't wait for the wedding day."

He paused again. "I found out on my wedding night that she wasn't a virgin. In fact, just a month after our marriage she told me she was pregnant with another man's child. 'We will just pretend that it's yours,' she said. 'We can say it came early. No one need know but the two of us.'"

I was stunned. This was something I had never expected. Then I was furious. How dare she do such a thing to Leo? It was a terrible trick to play on any man, but to Leo—whose son would be the next earl—it would be a devastating blow. How dare she do that to him?

"*Le Putain!* I said furiously. "Why did you not denounce her and put her away?"

A smile flickered when I called her a whore. He walked slowly up the rocky edge of the river and lowered himself to sit beside me. "I didn't do anything because I was very young and very humiliated. I did consider telling my father, but he was so full of plans for the new house, he had already started to build on the property that had come to him as part of Catherine's dowry." He shook his head slowly. "I just couldn't."

"Did she tell you who the father was?"

"She didn't know," he said and the bitterness in his voice made me wince. "She said it quite calmly, as if it were a triviality. She had been with four or five men and she didn't know which one was the father."

"Oh Leo." I reached out and took his hand. My heart was breaking for him. For something like this to happen to Leo! One of the best and kindest men who walked the earth! It was abominable. It was unspeakable. I held his hand against my cheek and said, "I hope she is burning in hell this, this *catin*, that you were forced to marry."

I felt his hand tense under my cheek. "There is something else I have to tell you, Isabel. Something about me that I still find hard to live with."

I moved his hand to my mouth, kissed it, and looked back at him. His expression was bleak. "When she—Catherine—began to have the baby, and the doctor came to tell me it was going to be a difficult delivery, that the baby wasn't positioned right, a terrible hope leaped inside me." I saw a muscle along his jaw twitch. "I hoped that she would die, Isabel. And when she did...when she did...I was glad."

He pulled his hand away from me. "I was glad. And when her baby died as well, I was glad about that too. I hated her, Isabel. I hated her so much that it had begun to corrode my soul. I swore that day that I would never marry again; I would never give another woman the chance to hurt me the way Catherine had." He paused, and when he spoke again his voice was quieter. "And then I met you."

Two emotions were fighting for control inside me. One was fury at the way he had been treated, and one was a need to help him, to reassure him he was not a bad person for having those feelings, that he was in fact the best man in the whole world. I leaned forward until I could slip my arms around him. I rested my head on his shoulder and said, "Most men in your position would have killed that woman. And she would have deserved it. You didn't ill wish her to her death, Leo. Her sin caught up with her. And *le pauvre bebe* is home with God."

His arms held me so tightly that I could scarcely breathe, but I didn't protest. The thought of Leo carrying this terrible burden of betrayal and guilt broke my heart. Leo! The golden boy. The sun child whose world always went his way. And all this time he had been hiding the pain of betrayal and guilt.

His mouth was next to my ear as he said, "Meeting you—it was like a cleansing wind had come into my life, blowing away all the debris of the past. For the first time in years I felt truly happy. I had this lovely, honest, enchanting girl in my life. But I had forced you to come to Camden. When I thought about it, I had virtually kidnapped you a second time. How could I think you would want to stay with me when your life in France had been so happy? I was afraid to speak to you; afraid I would drive you away from me if I did. But the fury I felt at Roger's daring to attack you, the relief I felt at having been in time to save you. I didn't think...I just acted." He paused, gave a short laugh, and said, "And now, here I am, trying to explain to you why I kissed you last night."

I said, "I would like to kill this Catherine. I would like to cut her up into little pieces and throw them to the dogs in my Papa's circus. She stole ten years of your life from you. She..."

I never got to finish that sentence because Leo's mouth came down on mine and before I knew it we were lying on the rough sand and I was so swamped by my emotions, by the feel of his hair under my fingers, the smell of his skin, the touch of his hand on my breast....

I don't know how we would have ended up if it weren't for the insistent whinnying of Alonzo. I was the one who heard him, and I struggled under Leo's weight. He rolled away immediately and we both looked at my horse, who was rolling his eyes, whinnying and snorting and pawing the ground.

I went to calm him with my heart still racing from Leo's touch. "What's wrong, boy?" I said soothingly. "Did you see a snake?" I was running my fingers along his neck under his mane. He seemed to be calming down.

Alonzo's alarm had infected Silver Boy and Leo was soothing his own horse. When both animals were grazing again Leo took my hand and moved us away from them. He said, "It's a good thing he distracted us. I don't know what would have happened if he hadn't. Just the feel of you under me was making me lose control."

I felt the blood rush into my face. He smiled and said softly, "Well, Isabel. What is your decision? Will you marry me?"

I couldn't answer. If I married Leo I would be deserting Papa. How could I do that? But how could I leave Leo? He was the man for me. My heart knew that. My body knew that. My whole being knew that. How could I give him up?

"Leo...what about my Papa? I don't think I can bear to leave him alone."

"I know that, sweetheart. And I know you have been worrying about him getting older and the circus being too much for him. I think I might have an answer that would suit the both of you."

"Tell me!"

He smiled and reached out to tuck a lock of loose hair behind my ear. "I've been thinking about this ever since I saw you ride at Astley's. As you point out to me all the time," one golden eyebrow arched, "we English don't know how to ride the way you do in France. We also don't have the kind of horses you have in France. What I would like to do is to create a stud here at Camden to breed the sort of horse suitable to your kind of equitation, and I would like to find a trainer to teach your sort of riding."

I stared at him, amazed. He had never said a word about this to me.

He continued, "I was hoping you would allow me to breed Alonzo to some appropriate mares, and I was hoping your father would act as my manager and trainer. Do you think he might be interested?"

"Yes!" I said immediately. "I think he would be very interested!" My brain was still trying to take in what Leo had said. Papa could live at Camden with us!

Leo put his hand under my chin and tipped my face up to his. His blue eyes held mine, and my heart leaped at the expression in them. "Under those circumstances, will you marry me Isabel?"

I opened my mouth to say *yes*, but what came out instead was, "Would you pay Papa a good salary?"

He started to laugh.

He was still tipping my face up to his. I tried not to smile, but I couldn't help it. I said, "I know. I know. The French and money."

"Everyone thinks of money, sweetheart," he said. "It's the French who are bold enough to admit their cupidity. And if your father will accept my offer, I will pay him a princely salary."

He was the most wonderful man in the world, and I was so happy I thought I just might float off the ground. "Yes," I said. "*Yes, yes, yes!* I love you with all my heart, Leo, and I will be happy to marry you."

He bent his face closer to mine. "May I kiss my fiancée?"

"You may," I replied.

Kissing Leo. I could spend the rest of my life just kissing Leo. His mouth covered mine and I leaned against him, loving the feel of his hard body against mine. He kept kissing me and kissing me, and when the force of his kisses bent my neck back, he put one hand behind my head to support it and the other hand came up to cover my breast. My heart was beating so hard I could feel it, and my knees were so weak that I had to lean harder against Leo to remain standing.

Then I was pushed out of paradise. I stood blinking up at Leo as he held me away from him. "God Almighty, Isabel, if this continues I can't answer for the consequences." His voice came out as a croak.

A lock of his hair had fallen across his forehead and I wanted to reach up and smooth it away but I knew that I shouldn't. Not yet at least.

The ride home was quiet. We neither of us felt the need to talk. Our bodies had spoken for us and that was enough for now.

Chapter Nineteen

The family, with the exception of Margaret, was gathered in the drawing room before dinner when Leo rose to his feet. He stood directly under the portrait of our great-grandmother as he said, "May I have everyone's attention? I have an important announcement to make."

My heart jumped and I cast a quick look around the room. Everyone was staring at Leo as if he was the archangel Gabriel sent down from heaven to impart a celestial message. Leo sent me a quick reassuring smile and I had to look down at my hands to hide my face. Mother, who had caught the smile, glanced at me in surprise.

Leo sounded as calm as if he were announcing a mere change in the dinner menu as he said, "I have asked Isabel to marry me and she has accepted. We have not yet sorted out the particulars of when or where, except that I want it to be soon."

He smiled at me again and my heart began to race so hard the ribbon on my bodice trembled.

Shocked silence greeted Leo's words; then everyone began to talk at once. My mother reached out and hugged me to her. "My dear, dear child," she said. "Nothing could have made me happier than this news." She released me reluctantly and smiled radiantly. There were tears in her eyes. "Now I will never lose you again."

The first voice to rise above the amazed exclamations belonged, of course, to Aunt Augusta. "Well done, Leo. We have become so fond of Isabel." And she looked at me and smiled.

I was stunned. I always thought she disapproved of me.

Everyone was standing up now, going up to Leo to shake his hand and coming to kiss my cheek. Over Aunt Jane's shoulder I caught a glimpse of Robert grinning at his brother and Leo grinning back. For a brief moment they looked like the small boys they must once have been.

Then my brother appeared in the doorway.

"What's this?" he asked as he entered the drawing room.

Every head snapped around. Leo took charge, saying pleasantly, "Ah Mansfield. You are in time to congratulate me. I have just announced that Isabel and I are to be married."

"Married?" My brother's face got very red as he looked from me to Leo. "You and Isabel? Oh no, Camden." His voice grew louder as he repeated, "No, No, and No. If you think you can cheat me out of my father's money by marrying Isabel, think again. I won't allow it!"

He was dressed for dinner in correct black coat and pantaloons, with his white neck cloth arranged in a stylish but restrained fashion. His long dark hair was brushed neatly back from his handsome face. He might be garbed in the clothes of a civilized man, but the expression on his face was savage. By the time he said, *"I won't allow it!"* he was shouting.

Leo lifted an eyebrow and replied in the same pleasant voice as before, "You have nothing to say in the matter, Mansfield."

"Oh yes I do! If Isabel is who you claim she is, she is my younger sister and under the law I am her guardian. She cannot marry anyone without my permission and I most definitely do not give my permission for her to marry you, Camden!"

At this I jumped to my feet. "You are not my guardian, you...you...*scelerat!*" I was so furious I struggled to get the words out. "If I want to marry Leo, I will. I do not need you to decide for me. I decide for myself!"

Henry's eyes narrowed as they met mine. "If you want to legally declare that you are not my sister, that will be fine with me. If you do that, you will have to give up all claims to the money my father left, and I will make no objection."

He looked from me to Leo and the expression on his face frightened me. He said, "I might have known you'd find a way to get your hands on my father's money, *Cousin.* You can marry her if you want but you'll have to present her to the world as a little circus girl with French peasants for parents. Because that's the only way you'll get to marry her, Leo. I can promise you that."

I was so furious I was shaking. "You will never get your hands on my money," I said in a trembling voice. "My father left it that way just so you could not have it. It belongs to me and I am going to give it to my Papa!"

Henry's eyes never moved from Leo. "You can't marry her any other way," he said. "I won't allow it."

He spun around and walked out of the room.

I ran to Leo. He put his arm around me and I pressed against his side. "He can't do what he says, can he?" I asked.

From behind me Aunt Augusta said, "You can't take this to the courts, Leo. Think of the scandal."

I felt Leo's lips gently touch my hair. "Don't let him upset you, Isabel. We'll find a way out of this, I promise."

Susan said, "You could just give the money to Mansfield, Isabel. If you're marrying Leo, you won't need it."

I stiffened and Leo's arm tightened around me. He said over my head, "I suggest we go into dinner and put this incident behind us. I promise you that Mansfield is not going to stop my marriage to Isabel, but you must leave the resolution of this problem to me."

We proceeded as usual into the dining room. Before we were served, however, Leo spoke to Hobbs. "I am sure you will be pleased to hear, Hobbs, that Lady Isabel has honored me by accepting my hand in marriage."

Hobbs almost dropped the wine glass he was holding. "Why...that is very good news, my lord." He gave me a lovely smile. "All of the staff will be delighted to know you will be remaining with us, Lady Isabel."

I smiled back. "Thank you, Hobbs."

He frowned at poor William who was standing next to the side table with his mouth open. William blushed and hurried to fill our glasses.

Conversation began with a discussion of the weather—a favorite English topic. As the conversation continued, I looked around the table. My English family might belong to a class I had been brought up to despise, but they were not like the French aristocrats who had deserved to have their heads cut off. In the time I had been at Camden Hall I had met Leo's tenants and seen their farms. Yes, his tenants worked hard, but they were well fed and well housed. Some of the families had worked the same farm for hundreds of years. The only difference between them and the farmers who lived around us in France was that the farmers I knew owned their land while Leo's tenants leased theirs. But Leo's tenants didn't have to worry about having to find the money for a new roof; all they had to do was ask Robert. I met my mother's eyes from across the table and I realized suddenly that I was proud to belong to such a family.

*

As usual we ladies retired to the drawing room leaving Leo, Robert and Sir John to their port. As soon as we were in the hallway, Susan grabbed my arm. "I have something I need to show you, Isabel," she said urgently. "It's in my room."

Aunt Augusta frowned. "Nonsense, Susan. What can you have to show Isabel? You cannot take her away from us on such an important occasion."

"We'll be right back, Aunt Augusta." Susan looked beseechingly at her mother.

"Let the girls have a little time to themselves," Aunt Jane said, smiling at Aunt Augusta. My mother agreed and Susan practically dragged me down the hallway.

"I don't have anything to show you, of course," she said when we were out of Aunt Augusta's hearing range. "Let's go to your sitting room. I want to know all about how you came to be engaged to Leo!"

There was no fire and my sitting room was chilly, but I kept some shawls there and handed one to Susan. We sat on the sofa, both of us huddled into the warm wool, and Susan said, "You never said a word to me about Leo and you!"

"You knew—everyone knew—that we were spending a lot of time together." I shrugged elaborately. "We got to know each other and to like each other and he asked me to marry him and I said yes."

Susan rolled her eyes. "Isabel, you have just landed the biggest catch on England's marriage mart. You must have more to say than that! He could have had anyone. Anyone. And he chose you! Aren't you thrilled?"

My voice was not quite steady as I answered, "If Leo were a French farmer, I would be thrilled. I know how to be a farmer's wife. I don't know how to be an earl's wife." I bit my lip and confided my misgiving to her. "I don't want to embarrass him by doing the wrong thing."

Susan said earnestly, "But don't you see, Isabel, that's why Leo fell in love with you. You're...well...you're different. You look at people and see the person, not the class. You'd rather spend time with Stoddard than with a duke! I am happy I'm the daughter of a viscount. You are happy you're the daughter of a circus owner. Leo loves you for who you are, Isabel."

I stared at the old blue wool rug, trying to grasp what Susan was telling me. She saw my confusion and reached over to take my hand. "There is something about you, Isabel—a vitality, a self-confidence, a *courage*—that is enormously attractive. It's what made Leo put aside his love for his lost wife and turn to you."

I thought about what Leo had told me about his "lost wife," and stifled the impulse to tell Susan the truth. Leo had trusted me, and I would never betray him. *I'd rather die*, I thought, dramatically perhaps, but honestly.

"Susan." I removed my eyes from the rug and looked at her. "Thank you." I felt tears coming to my eyes and didn't even try to blink them away. "You are a good friend. Thank you for helping me."

"You're welcome, Isabel. I think you're perfectly splendid and I'm so glad you're marrying Leo. We all love him, you know." Her face became solemn. "There is, however, one aspect of this marriage that you should consider carefully before you go through with it."

I blinked. After all she had said… "What is it?" I asked nervously.

"You will have to live with Aunt Augusta."

It took a moment for her words to register in my brain, but when they did I laughed. "I did think of that, and I am prepared to suffer Aunt Augusta," I said. "For Leo."

A soft knock sounded on the door and Freddy, one of the footmen, put his head around it. "I am sorry to bother you, my lady, but Lady Augusta sent me to ask you to come to the drawing room."

Susan and I gave each other meaningful looks.

"*For Leo,*" we said together, laughed, and prepared to return to the rest of the family.

Chapter Twenty

The day after Leo's announcement he and I drove into Lambourn to see James Sinclair, the solicitor who was in charge of the trust my father had left for me. I had accompanied Leo on a previous visit to Mr. Sinclair when Leo had directed the solicitor to file whatever paperwork was necessary to establish my legal identity.

We had no appointment this day, but the moment Leo walked into the waiting room we were escorted past the people sitting there and into the inner sanctum of the solicitor's office. Mr. Sinclair was a frail, elderly man, but his voice was deep and strong when he greeted us. After we were seated Leo exchanged pleasantries with the solicitor while I glanced around the room. There was scarcely any plaster showing as three of the walls were lined with packed bookcases. The fourth wall sported a painting of a spaniel. The room smelled of tobacco and, as before, I saw a wooden pipe on the desk.

The pleasantries done with, Leo said, "I have asked Lady Isabel to marry me and she has accepted."

Mr. Sinclair's brown eyes opened wide in surprise and, after a tiny pause, he began to offer Leo congratulations. Leo thanked him and said, "We are here because a problem has arisen. Lord Mansfield has informed me that since Lady Isabel has not yet reached the age of majority, he as her elder brother, has authority over her decisions. He has further stated that he will not give his permission for the marriage unless Lady Isabel gives up her rights to the trust and turns the money over to him."

Mr. Sinclair had been listening intently and now he leaned back in his chair, tenting his narrow hands in front of his chest. "This is interesting news, my lord, particularly since Lord Mansfield called here a few weeks ago to inform me he did *not* believe that the young woman residing at Camden Hall was his sister. He intimated that she might be a by-blow of some other member of the Sommer family and not connected to the Mansfields at all. Given that she was an imposter, he insisted that the trust money belonged to him."

Leo's hand closed into a fist, but he didn't say anything.

The solicitor continued, "I told him I believed there was sufficient evidence to testify to Lady Isabel's legitimacy. There was your evidence about the discussion you had with her foster father, which clearly points to the likelihood of Lady Isabel's birth. There is also her extraordinary resemblance to the portrait of your great-grandmother, and the fact that your family has so warmly embraced her. I told Lord Mansfield it would be very expensive to try to overturn the trust and he would most certainly fail in the end. You are well known for the acuteness of your brain, my lord, and there are very few who will believe you have been duped."

I glanced at Leo. His profile looked set in stone.

The solicitor spread his hands. "And now you are telling me Lord Mansfield has changed his mind and believes that Lady Isabel is his sister after all?"

"Yes. He's found another way to get his hands on the trust money. I do not want Lord Mansfield to have this money, Mr. Sinclair. It was intended for Lady Isabel and it should be given to her."

"I agree with you, my lord. But if we have Lady Isabel legally proclaimed to be Charlotte Lewins, the child who was stolen from the Earl and Countess of Mansfield, then I am afraid that, as her elder brother, Lord Mansfield will be her legal guardian."

"Is there no way we can get that changed?" Leo asked.

"I will be happy to look into the matter, my lord, but I must tell you that I do not think Lord Mansfield is incorrect in his belief that as Lady Isabel's older brother he will be able to dictate her marriage."

I had been slowly simmering during this conversation and now I said, "This is outrageous! My Papa is my guardian, not this Lord Mansfield whom I do not know. I am nineteen years of age! I am perfectly capable of deciding whom I want to marry. I don't need a guardian to tell me what I can or cannot do!"

Leo's big warm hand closed over mine. I hadn't realized I was gripping the chair arm so hard my knuckles were white.

"I don't doubt your capability, Lady Isabel," Mr. Sinclair said. "Unfortunately, however, the law does."

We left his office in mutual silence. Frankie, Leo's groom, was waiting in the street with the phaeton and horses. Leo lifted me up, Frankie jumped into the seat behind, Leo lifted the reins and we started for home.

Neither of us spoke. I stared through the ears of the carriage horse on my side of the phaeton and made an effort to consider my situation rationally. It seemed to me that there was only one solution to this problem. We had to legally establish that I was *not* Charlotte Lewins, that I was Isabel Besson and the Earl of Mansfield had no say in what I might choose to do.

I said this to Leo, and he shot me a blazing blue look. "I will *never* allow you to renounce your heritage! The blood of generations of English nobles runs in your veins. I will never allow Mansfield to win on this issue." He shot me another look. "If we do as you suggest, you'll lose the trust money. Have you thought about that?"

A small muscle was twitching in his jaw, his mouth was set into a hard line and his cheekbones looked more prominent than usual. He was furious.

I had never seen Leo angry before and it was intimidating. But I wasn't ready to give up. "I don't give a fig for what kind of blood is in my veins. As long as it's red and it keeps me alive, I am happy to have it. Let my hateful brother keep the money. All I care about is being married to you."

I had spoken instinctively, but I meant what I said. Mr. Sinclair was too certain about Henry's rights in regard to me. If I had to give my brother the money in order to marry Leo, then I would give him the money. Leo would see to it that Papa was provided for.

I said as much to Leo and only succeeded in making him angrier. "That money belongs to you and I am going to make certain that you get it. Leave this problem of Mansfield to me, Isabel. I will resolve it."

"But how?"

He shot me another of those looks and said, spacing his words, *"You will get your money, we will be married in my parish church, and you will take your proper place as Lady Camden. My wife."*

I have always thought of myself as brave, but I didn't want to argue with him. I kept my silence and he kept his. It was an uncomfortable ride home.

*

When the phaeton stopped in front of the house Robert came out the front door as if he had been watching for us. He went immediately to Leo, who had jumped down from the phaeton's high seat, and said something I couldn't hear. Then the two of them came around to my side and Leo lifted me down. I was perfectly capable of jumping down myself, but I liked the feel of Leo's hands around my waist, so I let him help me.

"Robert tells me we have a visitor we should attend to immediately," Leo said as we walked toward the front door.

"A visitor? Who?"

"A friend of mine. Come along and I'll introduce you."

He was trying to be mysterious, but my mind was too full of what Mr. Sinclair had said to pay much attention. I had bigger things to think about than an unexpected guest.

I stepped into the drawing room doorway and saw a slim man standing by the window. The light shone upon his hair—he had always been proud of his thick hair—and his gray eyes were fixed upon the doorway. My heart leaped. *"Papa!"* I screamed and ran toward him.

Chapter Twenty-One

I threw myself into Papa's embrace and only stepped back when Leo said, "I would like to shake your father's hand, Isabel. Do you think you might let go of him for a moment?"

I loosened my grip on Papa so Leo could shake his hand. "I hope you have not been waiting long," Leo said courteously. "Did they give you something to eat and drink?"

"Yes," Papa replied in his careful English. He gestured toward one of the small gilt tables that stood next to the brocade sofa; it held a teacup and a plate.

I took Papa's hand and held it tightly. "How did you get here? Did you come by yourself? Who is running the circus? What is...?"

Papa cut into my barrage of questions. "Isabel, Isabel, do not be so hasty. I will answer your questions, but one at a time please."

Leo, who was standing behind me, said, "Why don't you take your father to your sitting room sweetheart? I'll have a bottle of wine sent along and some of your favorite biscuits."

I turned away from Papa and gave Leo a smile that trembled with emotion. I tugged on Papa's hand and said, "Leo has given me my own private sitting room in the medieval part of the house. It's totally different from this part—cozier I think. Wait until you see it."

We walked down Camden's magnificent hallway, went through the door that led to the medieval part of the house and established ourselves in my familiar little sitting room. We sat next to each other on the sofa and I laid my cheek against his arm so I could sniff his familiar smell. He turned and took me in his arms. *Papa is here!* I thought. *Papa is really here!*

A footman knocked on the door and delivered a tray holding a wine bottle, two glasses, and a plate of pastries. Once Papa and I had toasted each other with the wine, he told me about how his unexpected arrival at Camden Hall in Berkshire, England, had come about.

"We were in the midst of a show on the outskirts of Deauville—you know the place, Isabel." I nodded that I did. "I was watching Madeleine perform with the liberty horses—I thought Magnus might be a bit off on the left hind—when a man came up to me and asked if I was Pierre Besson. I said I was, and he handed me an envelope. The messenger said, "It is from the Earl of Camden, Monsieur. He asks that you read it and give me an answer.""

"Leo sent you a letter?" I was astonished. "He never said a word to me about it." I shifted my position so I could see Papa's face better. "What did it say?"

"He told me that you had agreed to marry him. And he asked me to come to England to be the horsemaster and manager of the new stud farm he was planning. He said his aim was to breed horses suitable for French-style equitation, and also to train English riders to ride them. He would pay me a handsome salary and give me a house of my own if I did not wish to live with his family. He invited me to come to England for your wedding and he told me that George Johnson, who had brought me this letter, was prepared with tickets for the boat to England. If I did not wish to accept his offer, he said that as soon as you were married, he would bring you to France to visit me."

When Papa stopped talking, he pulled a piece of paper from his pocket and offered it. "Here is the letter. I think you should read it."

It was a beautiful letter. Leo said such lovely things about me and told Papa how much he loved me and wanted to take care of me for the rest of our lives. He made his offer to Papa sound as if Papa would be doing him a great favor if he would accept the position Leo was offering. Even if Papa did not wish to leave the circus, Leo asked him to return with George for a visit because *your daughter misses you very much, Monsieur, and I fear she will not marry me unless you are present.*

Tears were running down my face when I handed the letter back. "He's such a wonderful man, Papa. He's kind and generous and caring of other people." I wiped the back of my hand across my wet cheeks and sniffed. "He's just like you."

Papa smiled. "Not exactly, little one. He is a very great lord in this country. He has much power. This earl is very much higher in the world than your little circus-owning Papa."

"I know that. And I worry that I won't be a good wife for him. I won't know how to behave when I have to go to London and meet his friends."

Papa cupped my face in his hands. "Do not cry, my little one. All you need to do is be yourself. The earl fell in love with the real you. That is who he wants you to be. Do not ever think of trying to change. The both of us love the girl that you are right now." He bent his head, kissed the tears on my cheeks and handed me a handkerchief.

I blew my nose.

"How is Alonzo?" he asked.

I brightened instantly and we sat talking for two hours, almost finishing the bottle of wine and all of the pastries. Papa was interested in the position Leo had offered, but worried about what would happen to the circus.

"Leon has been by your side for years, Papa," I said. "He could run the circus. You know he could. He ran it when we were at Astley's, didn't he?"

Papa didn't try to dispute Leon's capability. Instead he said sadly, "Leon has not the money to buy the circus, Isabel. I have paid him a generous salary, but the circus is worth far more than he could have saved."

"You can give him the circus, Papa," I urged. "Leo will be giving you a house and a big salary. And I may be coming into some money from the estate of my birth father. You won't need money from Leon. And we will be together!"

Papa's eyes bulged. "*Give* Leon the circus! Are you mad, Isabel? The Cirque Equestre is worth a great deal of money. People all over France wait for us to arrive in their town. We are the big event of their summers. Even the people from the chateaux come to see us. We take in large sums of money." He shook his head in incredulity. "We are beloved all over France and you want me to *give* the circus to Leon? *Non*, that I cannot do."

We argued until we had finished the bottle of wine. I plunked my empty glass on the old oak table that sat before the sofa and said, "Fine. Then go back to France and continue with the circus. Obviously you won't miss me."

He was horrified. "Of course I will miss you, little one. I have missed you terribly these last few months when I was in France and you were here. I have missed you more than you will ever know." Tears glimmered in his eyes. Wine always made Papa sentimental.

I removed the empty glass from his hand, laid it on the table and took both his hands into mine. "Then stay with me, Papa. Leo has made you a splendid offer. You will be making more money than you ever have, and you won't have to keep traveling. And the English need your help, Papa. They really are terrible riders."

He laughed at that, his beloved face, so deeply lined from the summer suns he had worked under for most of his life, crinkled in the way I loved. "Let me speak to the earl, little one. Then I will make up my mind."

Time flew and when the bell rang to alert us to dress for dinner, I was surprised. Papa started for the door, but I put my hand on his arm and held him in place. He looked at me with raised eyebrows.

I lowered my voice. "Papa, I must warn you. The food here is terrible. I have got used to it a little—when one is hungry any food looks good. But they overcook everything!"

"That does not sound appetizing," he said. He looked down at his garments. "How do these people dress? I'm sure I will look very shabby to them, but there is nothing to be done about it."

Papa was wearing a dark blue wool coat, fawn-colored breeches and light-brown cotton stockings. He had on his best black leather shoes with the silver buckles. "I have my good blue coat with me, Isabel, and my silk stockings," he assured me.

"You will look just fine," I assured him staunchly. I bit my lip, then decided I had better prepare him for what was to come.

"You won't believe the fuss they make about dinner here, Papa. We all dress as if we're going to the opera and we march into the dining room in a line. It's quite amusing. And please ignore whatever Aunt Augusta might say. She has no manners."

"Aunt Augusta. She is the maiden aunt you mentioned in your letters."

"Yes. I think she'll behave herself. Leo will have spoken to her."

I put my hand on the door handle to open it, but Papa stopped me. "Are you sure about this marriage, Isabel? You are not marrying the earl for my sake? There is no need to worry about me, little one. I have money set aside from all the years we have performed. I own the farm. I do not need any of the earl's money."

I smiled at him. "I am marrying him because I love him, Papa. I never dreamed I could love a man as much as I love Leo. If only you would join us here at Camden, I would be the happiest girl in the whole world."

"*Bien*. That is what I wanted to hear. Now, come, let us get dressed for dinner so I can meet this Aunt Augusta."

Chapter Twenty-Two

Papa's first dinner with the family went well. His English was good enough for him to join the conversation occasionally, and his comments were always resonant with his native good sense. Surprisingly, Aunt Augusta seemed quite taken with him. As we ladies left the table to adjourn to the drawing room, she remarked that it was fortunate I had come into the hands of such an admirable man!

Two days after Papa's arrival, Leo mentioned at dinner he would be leaving for London the day after tomorrow. He had some business to attend to and he hoped to be back by early the following week.

He had said nothing to me about London. I looked at him as he sat there in all his splendid male beauty and thought, *He has a mistress in London. Is he going to see her? Is he going to stay with her? If he thinks I will tolerate that kind of behavior he is very much mistaken.*

We ladies retired to the drawing room as usual, but I was so tightly wound I think I would have pinged if someone touched me. Tea was brought in and Aunt Augusta poured. Leo had still not come in nor had Papa. When I asked Robert where they were he said the billiard room. I knew Papa liked to play billiards and normally I would be happy to see my father and my future husband getting acquainted. But not tonight.

I waited in the drawing room until all the ladies had retired. Then I sent one of the footmen to the billiard room with a written message for Leo. *I must speak with you. Come to the drawing room. Alone. I will be waiting.*

I waited for thirty minutes, getting more and more furious. Finally the drawing room door opened and Leo came in. He held up my note. "What is this about, Isabel?"

I struggled to sound calm as I replied, "I was surprised when you announced tonight you were going to London. I was wondering what kind of business was so important that you had to leave so quickly."

He took another step towards me. "I want to consult with my London solicitor about our situation with Mansfield. He is very astute and might be able to find a way out of this guardianship obstacle your brother has thrown up. I also have some friends who might be able to help."

It was a very sensible reply. "Will you be staying at your townhouse while you are in London?" I asked, struggling to remain calm.

"No, I'll stay at my club. There's no sense in opening up the townhouse for just a few days."

"Oh." I didn't know if his staying at his club was a good thing or a bad thing.

His brows lifted. "Why did you want to know about the townhouse?"

I inhaled deeply. "Because I don't want you to stay with your mistress."

He could not have looked more stunned if I had slapped him across the face. "How do you know about my mistress?"

"Everyone knows." I held his gaze and did not blink.

"Everyone knows?" He was still looking stunned. "Well then," he demanded, his stunned look turning to anger, "who was idiot enough to tell *you*?"

I had no intention of betraying Susan. "That's not important. What's important is that I do not want a husband who has a mistress! You need to get rid of her." I stepped closer and glared up at him. "Is she still living in the house you are paying for?"

He let out a long breath and with it his anger dissipated. "The other reason I am going to London is to tell Helena that I am to be married and will be breaking off our relationship."

This was excellent news, but I still didn't like the idea of them meeting. "Why can't you just write to her?"

"I must speak to her to make certain she has a place to live and enough money to live on once we separate. It would be unkind to let her find out about our marriage from the newspaper."

"I hope you're not planning to sleep with her."

His eyes got very blue. "Is that what you were thinking?"

"I'm French," I said. "I have a suspicious mind."

At that he reached out and pulled me into his arms. "I promise that you will never have to worry about another woman, my darling. You are more than enough woman for me."

My cheek was against his shoulder and I inhaled the clean, male smell of him. I felt very happy. "Look at me, Isabel," he commanded. I lifted my face and his lips met mine. I slid my arms around him so that my body was pressed along the length of his. I loved being in his arms. I could stay like this forever, I thought, as delicious tremors began to make themselves felt in many different parts of my body.

Leo clearly didn't feel the same way because he grabbed my shoulders and lifted me away from him. I looked up to protest, but the expression in his eyes stopped me.

"I love kissing you," I said.

"I love kissing you too, Isabel. But what I really want is to get you in bed." His eyes were narrowed and dark. His voice was hoarse.

"I want that too," I said. "Do we really have to wait until we are married? What can a few weeks matter?"

He shut his eyes. "Dear God, Isabel, do not tempt me like this!" He opened his eyes. "Yes, we have to wait until we're married. I do not want to get you with child before, and we might have to wait before this situation with Mansfield is resolved."

"We won't have to wait if I give the money to him."

"No. That money is yours and you shall have it if I have to murder him to get it."

"I want that money, yes. But I want to marry you more! I know you will take care of Papa. He would never take money from you gratuitously, but he will accept your offer to establish a stud and a riding school here at Camden. He is thrilled by it, in fact. He will never admit it, but I suspect he was getting tired of the circus. He was reluctant to leave home this year when the season opened. A few years ago, he couldn't wait to get back to circus life, but now I think he finds the constant traveling a hardship."

He smiled at me and touched my cheek with his forefinger. "While it's nice to hear that I'm more important to you than the money, I am not ready yet to give it up. That's why I want to talk to some people about the situation, to see if they might have some suggestions."

I was hoping he would kiss me again, but he just told me to go to bed then he stood at the bottom of the stairs watching me until I was out of sight.

*

Leo had said he would be away for a few days, but the few days turned into a week. I didn't hear from him and I couldn't help but think of that mistress. I trusted Leo. Of course I trusted Leo. But I wished he would come home.

Leo was still away on the day I received a shocking visit. I was riding Alonzo in the ring for Papa when Lawrence, the youngest footman, appeared. Footmen rarely came to the stable area, and I brought Alonzo down to a walk and looked over the fence at Lawrence, who was uncomfortably out of place in his white wig and buckled shoes. "Do you have a message for me?" I asked.

"Yes, Lady Isabel. Lady Hepburn asked that you return to the house as soon as possible."

My heart dropped into my stomach. "Has something happened to his lordship?"

"I don't know, my lady. I was just sent to deliver the message."

I dismounted. Papa had come over to stand beside me and I asked him to take Alonzo back to the stable before he returned to the house. He patted me on the shoulder and told me to go.

My mind was churning. My mother would not have interrupted my ride if it weren't something important. Perhaps Leo had returned!

"Lady Hepburn is in the blue salon," Hobbs said as I entered the hallway.

I went down the hall, my boots clicking on the marble tile, and walked into the salon. Sir John and a man I didn't know stood as I approached them. My mother and Aunt Jane were seated on the sofa. Mother reached out her hand. "Come and sit here, my love. This is Sir William Wolcott, our local magistrate. He has some sad news for us."

I felt the blood drain from my face. "Is it Leo? Has something happened to Leo?"

"No darling. Leo is fine. Come and sit; you look as if you might faint."

Sir John had a supporting hand under my elbow. "I never faint," I said, and allowed Sir John to guide me to the sofa.

When I was seated, and Mother had patted my hand, Sir John said, "Isabel, Sir William Wolcott has some news to impart."

Sir William was the local squire, a robust man with a broad weathered face. He said, "I am sorry to have to tell you that your brother was shot to death early this morning, Lady Isabel.

It happened while Lord Mansfield was taking his usual morning ride through the estate woods. He was riding with a friend who was staying with him and the friend states he saw someone afoot in the woods right before he heard the shot. Mr. Forsythe—the friend—couldn't give chase because he had to help his lordship."

My first reaction was shock. Then the happy thought came. *Henry's death means he can't claim to be my guardian.*

"How awful," I said weakly.

The squire continued, "Considering the circumstances, Mr. Forsythe rightly sent for the magistrate. I came immediately and observed that his lordship had been shot in the head."

That information truly shocked me. I don't know why, but the image of someone shot in the head is horrific.

"I gave orders for the body to be taken to the estate icehouse," the squire said. "I will inform the coroner. There will have to be an inquest."

"It was obviously a poacher," Sir John said.

"From what Mr. Forsythe has told me, I have ruled that possibility out. No poacher deliberately takes aim at a human person. Also, it was too late in the morning for poachers to be out."

Aunt Jane said in a bewildered voice, "Who on earth would be such a fool as to shoot an earl? I can't imagine that Mansfield could have made himself that hated."

It hit me like an arrow to the heart. Leo had a motive. But no one else knew about the guardianship issue except Mr. Sinclair! I relaxed infinitesimally. Leo was safe.

The squire said, "Is his lordship at home, my lady?"

My heart jumped. "His lordship is in London. We expect him home any time now."

"Are you certain he is still in London?" The squire wore an expression I did not like. He looked...eager.

"Yes." Then I added in Aunt Augusta's haughtiest tone, "What can his lordship have to do with this shooting?"

"I asked because Lord Camden is the only person I know who has a reason to see Lord Mansfield dead."

"What!" Sir John leaped to his feet. "How dare you make such an accusation, sir? I must ask you to leave this house immediately."

"Wait," I said in a constricted voice. "I would like to hear what kind of motive Sir William thinks Leo has."

"Lord Mansfield was blocking your marriage to Lord Camden, Lady Isabel. He was going to assert his rights as your legal guardian and forbid you to marry his lordship. I would call that a motive."

I stared at him in shock. Leo and I had told no one, not even my mother. "Where did you get such an absurd idea?" I tried for outraged indignation.

"You didn't quite close the door when you were speaking to Mr. Sinclair and one of the people in the waiting room has very keen ears. He will be willing to swear to what he heard." The squire stood up and stared directly into my eyes. "Tell his lordship when he arrives home that I would like to speak with him"

Sir John said grimly, "I will show you out," and the two men left the room.

Chapter Twenty-Three

Everyone left in the room looked at me. "Is this true, Isabel?" My mother was clearly upset. I didn't know if it was because of the squire's news or because I hadn't told her. It was probably both.

"Yes, it's true." I inhaled deeply, looked steadily at the riding skirt that covered my lap and related the gist of our visit to Mr. Sinclair. "That's why Leo went to London," I concluded. "He wanted to consult with some solicitors there to see if we could overturn this hideous guardianship rule."

What I didn't do was repeat Leo's words to me when we learned about the guardianship: *That money is yours and you shall have it even if I have to murder him.*

I didn't say the words, but they reverberated loudly in the back of my mind.

"I don't like this." It was Sir John who had come back into the room. "I don't like the way that man went after Leo. A man of Wolcott's status doesn't challenge an earl the way this man did Leo."

Aunt Jane agreed. "It's almost as if there was something personal involved."

"Leo is safely in London," my mother said stoutly. "Any suspicion of him must be put to rest when it becomes obvious he was miles away."

Mother was right. I had been wishing Leo at home but now I wished the opposite. Please God, I prayed, let Leo stay in London for at least another day!

*

That very afternoon, as the family was gathered in the drawing room for tea, Leo arrived home.

Oh no, I thought, as I stared at my golden-haired beloved in the doorframe. *Not today, Leo. Why did you come home today?*

The entire family was staring at him too, probably thinking the same thing. I stood, went up to him, tipped my head, smiled and said, "Welcome home."

"It's about time." Aunt Augusta hadn't been told about the squire's visit and she sounded perfectly normal. "What have you been doing all this time, Leo? We have a wedding to think of. Did you at least send notice of the marriage to the newspaper?"

While Aunt Augusta was speaking Leo was kissing me. I wanted so much to throw my arms around him, to hold him close, to feel his warm strength next to me. But I couldn't do that in front of the entire family. I forced myself to step away and say, "There's room for you on the tapestry sofa."

He came with me to the sofa and sat between me and Robert. Susan said, "I'll bring you a cup of tea, Leo. Would you like a scone?"

He looked at the uneaten scone on my plate. Then he looked at me. He raised one golden eyebrow. His blue eyes looked right into mine. "You haven't eaten your scone, Isabel."

He knew how hungry I always was at teatime.

"I am planning to," I said.

The blue eyes narrowed. I knew he wouldn't ask me anything personal in front of the family, so I smiled brightly, took a bite and forced myself to chew. Susan arrived with tea and a scone for Leo. He looked at all the gazes fixed on him and said. "All right. Something has happened while I was away. You had better tell me about it. I promise not to faint."

We all looked at Robert. He knew his duty and said, "Mansfield was murdered this morning. He was shot from his horse while he was riding through his own woods. The friend who was with him, a fellow called Forsythe, said he saw a man in the woods running away. He couldn't go after him since he had to attend to Mansfield, who had been shot in the head."

"Good God." I was watching Leo and he looked genuinely stunned. "Had he been having problems with poachers?"

Robert shook his head. "We all have to deal with poachers on occasion, but I simply cannot imagine a poacher having the nerve to kill an earl. And a shot to the head? It doesn't make sense."

Leo agreed.

"The squire was called in as magistrate," Robert continued, "and he had the nerve to come here to Camden to ask some damn fool questions about you. Tell him, Isabel. You were in the room."

I tried to speak calmly as I explained the situation. "Sir William was interested in your whereabouts, Leo. Too interested. He sounded suspicious. It was very strange. I assured him that you were still in London and we didn't know when you would return."

Leo frowned deeply but remained quiet.

Aunt Augusta said, "Why wasn't I informed of this? The nerve of that man, coming here and accusing the Earl of Camden of shooting a man! Who does the squire think he is, behaving in such an outrageous fashion?"

"It is very strange," my mother said.

"Who was in the room with him beside you?" Leo asked me.

"Mother. Sir John. Aunt Jane."

"What did you think, Sir John?" Leo asked my mother's husband.

"I thought it was damn offensive. The man clearly intimated that you were a suspect. He offered no reason for his suspicion, but he was too certain for my comfort."

"Wolcott doesn't like me," Leo said. "If he could do me a mischief he would."

"Doesn't like you?" I echoed. "How can anyone not like *you?*"

His eyes softened as he looked down at me. "Not everyone thinks I am as wonderful as you do, sweetheart."

"Are you talking about that business when you first came into the title?" Robert asked.

"What business?" Aunt Augusta demanded.

Leo's answer was directed to me. "The Earls of Camden have long held the responsibility of Lord Lieutenant of the County, Isabel, and in England that role holds a certain judicial power. When my father died, I was appointed Lord Lieutenant by the King." I nodded my understanding. "My father had appointed Wolcott to be the local magistrate, a post the local squire often holds. Shortly after I came into the title, a breech of justice by the magistrate was brought to my attention. I'm not going to go into the particulars, but I ruled that Wolcott had acted irresponsibly in charging a fifteen-year-old tenant of mine of poaching. He wanted to have the boy sent to Australia as punishment. I thought the punishment was extreme and when I learned that the boy had got into a round of fisticuffs with Wolcott's son and Wolcott's son had got the worst of it, I gave the boy a good talking to and let him go. Wolcott has neither forgot nor forgiven me for it."

My mother said staunchly, "I agree with Isabel, Leo. I cannot imagine anyone would believe you capable of murder."

Leo said, "Thank you, Aunt Maria. I had better send word to Wolcott that I have returned. I will be interested to learn the reason why he holds me in suspicion."

I braced myself to tell him that the squire knew about our session with Mr. Sinclair, but Robert spoke first. "What time did you leave London this morning? If you were in London, you could not have been here shooting Mansfield."

Leo let out a long breath. "Well I wasn't in London this morning, Rob. I stopped over at Harry Dean's for the night."

"Who is this Harry Dean person?" Aunt Augusta demanded.

"An old school friend. We ran into each other in London and he invited me to stop at his house for some shooting before I came home."

"Well then, Dean can vouch for you being at his house this morning," Robert said.

Leo let out another long breath. "I left Harry's early because I wanted to get home. What time did this shooting take place?"

"About ten o'clock in the morning, I believe."

Leo held Robert's eyes. He looked very somber. "I could have made it back in time to shoot Mansfield, Rob."

"But you just got here!" I protested. "Where does this Harry Dean live that it took you so long?"

"Dean's home is just outside of Newbury. I left at seven in the morning. I could easily have made it back here by ten o'clock. I was late because Walter threw a shoe. I had to walk for an hour before I found a blacksmith, and when I did find a forge the blacksmith wasn't there. He was out shoeing horses at a local farm so I had to wait for him to return. Then I was held up again when Walter decided the shoe wasn't fitting his hoof properly and went lame. So I had to find another blacksmith and have the shoe redone. It was not a pleasant journey."

"You must be starved, poor boy," Aunt Augusta said. "Susan, bring Leo some more scones."

Leo's hunger is the least of our problems, I thought with alarm. If I didn't know him, I'd think his story of the troublesome horseshoe sounded questionable.

Rob said, "If necessary, the two blacksmiths could vouch for you, could they not?"

"I suppose so," Leo said. "If it becomes necessary."

Robert put a hand on his brother's arm. "If we can discover who actually did murder Mansfield, you wouldn't need witnesses at all." Robert's hand tightened on Leo's sleeve. "Who profits most from Mansfield's death?"

Leo shrugged.

Robert said firmly, "His heir profits. Whoever is Mansfield's heir inherits an earldom."

"An earldom on the edge of bankruptcy I should think," Leo returned.

"He wouldn't know about Mansfield's financial state. Do we know who the heir is?"

We all looked at Aunt Augusta. She said promptly, "The heir is a first cousin of Mansfield's—his father's brother's son. All I know about him is that his father—Mansfield's uncle—

married a woman his father disapproved of. They have been cut off from the family ever since."

"He'll be at the funeral," Robert said. "Once we find out who he is we can look into his financial affairs. The man might have been short of money himself and thought to inherit a fortune if Mansfield died."

I thought this was an excellent idea and congratulated Robert for thinking of it.

*

Before dinner Leo and I managed to snatch a few minutes alone in my sitting room. We sat side by side on the comfortable old sofa and I turned to ask him a question. "No talking," he said, and his mouth came down on mine. His kiss was more intoxicating than any wine could be. As he felt me respond he deepened the kiss. My lips parted and his tongue came between them. He leaned me back against the soft pillow on the end of the sofa and I lifted my hand to run my hand through the golden thickness of his hair. It felt so crisp and strong. Everything about Leo was strong.

His hand moved to my breast and I was shocked by the spasm of pleasure that ran through my body at that touch. I gasped, and Leo moved away.

I sat up and put the tips of my fingers on my lips. Leo was sitting at the far end of the sofa, his hands on his knees and his head bent. I could see the movement of his chest.

I waited for him to compose himself. Finally he looked up, gave me a crooked smile and said, "Will you please plan this wedding?"

I smiled back and said, "I'll speak to Mother."

Chapter Twenty-Four

I went down to breakfast early and was shocked to find Aunt Augusta there before me. I said her name in surprise as I went to the table where the muffins were laid out. "Why are you up so early?"

"I could not sleep last night," she said. "I am concerned about Leo's possible connection to this murder."

"He didn't do it…" I began but she interrupted me. "Of course he didn't do it! Leo is far too decent a man to sully his hands with murder."

"I agree." I allowed William to fill my coffee cup. English tea was all right in the afternoon but not in the morning.

"I shall be attending the funeral with you tomorrow," Aunt Augusta announced.

I returned my muffin to the plate and looked across the table at her. But Aunt Augusta…your back. Won't the carriage ride be too painful for you?"

"I know my duty," she replied austerely. "We have a connection to that family, and as the oldest living member of our family I feel it is my duty to attend."

"I see." It was all I could think to say. Aunt Augusta never went anywhere. I wondered if she also wanted to meet Henry's heir.

I sipped my coffee in silence and Aunt Augusta ate two sausages. When she had finished, she said, "Once this funeral is over, we must begin to plan the wedding."

I sighed. "Do we need to have a large wedding? I would love to be married with just the family present. It would be much more personal."

She put down her fork and regarded me frostily. "This wedding isn't for you, it's for Leo. As the Earl of Camden, he has certain social obligations, and this is one of them. The tenants and townsfolk will be expecting and looking forward to a big wedding. You must understand Isabel that Leo is beloved by the people of Camden. He is good to his tenants and he purchases almost all of the supplies for his house and stables from local people. These people want to see him married. They want to see him happy. And we must oblige them."

"I understand," I said softly. "It is nice to hear how beloved Leo is in the countryside."

"He is a good man," Aunt Augusta said in a voice I had never heard before. "He has housed his officious old aunt for years and never once made her think she was a burden."

I felt tears sting behind my eyes at these words. I blinked them back and smiled. "You have been very helpful to me, Aunt Augusta, and I appreciate it. I hope I can count on your advice in the future. I don't have any experience in running a house this size."

Her eyes brightened. "I shall be happy to advise you, Isabel. Please don't hesitate to come to me at any time."

"I won't," I said.

The two of us finished our breakfasts in peaceful accord.

*

The funeral took place the following day. Aunt Augusta was going to stay over at Mansfield Park in order not to make the coach journey twice in one day, and Aunt Jane had volunteered to stay with her. They came in the carriage with Leo and me. Since Mansfield Park was only eleven miles away, Leo would send the carriage back for them tomorrow.

Mother and Sir John drove in their own coach and, since it was a fine day, Robert and Margaret went in the phaeton.

I felt like such a hypocrite as I walked behind the black carriage that was carrying Henry's casket to the church. The procession was impressive. Four black horses with black plumes on their heads drew the carriage, and a gathering of black-clad mourners followed behind us. Mother and Sir John walked beside Leo and me. Robert, Margaret and Aunt Jane walked behind. I wondered if they felt like hypocrites too.

After the church service the family was expected to accompany the casket to its final resting place while the rest of the entourage went back to the house for food and drink. I watched as some workers lowered Henry into the grave and I shivered. I thought about death and how it can be so unexpected, so unprepared for. Being young was no protection. A bullet had struck down Henry; a disease had struck down my mother. It was important to seize happiness and cherish it while you had it.

I am so fortunate I thought as we turned away from the grave and Leo put his arm around my shoulders. I turned my cheek into the black wool of his coat and closed my eyes. I have Leo, I thought. I have Papa. I have Mother. *Please, God, I prayed. Keep us all safe.*

We stayed for a short time at the small reception that was held in the drawing room. To the huge disappointment of all of us from Camden, the new heir turned out to be a thirteen-year-old boy. His father, who had been Henry's first cousin, had died recently from pneumonia. Obviously neither father nor son had shot Henry.

The evening was coming on by the time we returned home. Susan grabbed me as soon as I came in the door wanting to know how the funeral had gone. She accompanied me to my room and established herself in the comfortable chair in front of the fireplace. I told her about the heir as Elisabeth helped me change into dinner clothes.

"A thirteen-year-old boy!" She was as stunned as we had been when we met James Lewins. "I hope he's nothing like Henry was when he was young."

"He seemed to be very nice, very young, and very overwhelmed. His mother told me he couldn't wait to go back to school."

"Was there much talk about the murder?"

"Not in the drawing room, but I'll wager there was a lot of talk on the back lawn." The lawn was where refreshments had been set up for the tenants and neighbors.

"How many of them attended? Mama says that Henry did nothing for his tenants and they all despised him."

"I heard one man saying to another that he felt obligated to eat and drink at the bastard's expense since Mansfield had done nothing to help put food in the mouths of his children. If this had been France he would have had his head cut off, which he richly deserved. Then someone else wouldn't have had to kill him."

"You don't mean that!" Susan said. I had learned that the English aristocracy were terrified by what had happened in France, and I thought my brother was a good example of just why our revolution had occurred.

I was dressed by now and Susan stood up to walk out with me. "Was there any talk about the murder?" she asked as we walked down the hallway.

I stopped and turned to her. "The story of our meeting with Mr. Sinclair has spread all over town. Everyone seemed to know about it." I was so furious my voice shook. "That *batard* Wolcott must have told everyone. I would like to shoot *him* in the head."

"I don't blame you," Susan said staunchly.

"The most frustrating thing was that while I knew people were talking about it, no one said anything to us. Leo told me to ignore the talk and act normally and I tried to do that." I drew a deep breath to calm myself. "One good thing did happen, though."

"What was that?"

"While we were waiting for our carriage to be brought around several of Leo's tenants came up to him and said he was not to worry, that no one believed he had shot Henry."

"What did Leo say?"

"He thanked them and said he hoped that others felt the same way. They said *everyone* believed in Leo's innocence. And"—I paused to emphasize this point—"the tenants also said that even if Leo had done it, they were still behind him, that everyone was happy to be rid of Lord Mansfield."

"Good for them!" Susan's eyes were sparkling. "It's not fair for Leo to be put in this position." She took my hand and squeezed it. "But isn't it wonderful that Mansfield is dead?"

I looked at her and we both grinned. "It is," I said. "It certainly is."

Susan said, "Now we can turn our attention to your wedding.

"Yes," I said. If a big wedding was what Leo needed, then I would help to give it to him.

Chapter Twenty-Five

The coroner arrived the day of the funeral and he called for an inquisition to take place the following day. Usually the bodies of those who died by sudden, violent or unnatural death were not allowed to be buried until after the coroner and the jury viewed the corpse. Because of Henry's elevated position the coroner had accepted the magistrate's description and allowed my brother's body to be decently buried.

The inquest was to be held in the taproom of the local tavern, as it was the only room big enough to hold the number of people expected to turn out. The hateful Wolcott sent a formal summons to Leo requiring him to attend.

Leo and I had just returned to the house from our ride and were eating our breakfast when Hobbs came in with the summons. Leo had not expected this, and he was furious. His face hardened, his eyes narrowed, and the classically perfect bones of his face stood out under his whitened skin. In a dangerously quiet voice he said, "I can't believe he has the audacity to do this. He knows, he must know, that I would never stoop so low. I would have found a way to get around Mansfield without having to murder him."

At this point Robert and Margaret came into the room. Robert took one look at Leo and said, "What has happened?"

"This has happened." Leo tossed the paper in Robert's direction.

"The bastard," Robert said, looking up from the summons. "You should remove him from office, Leo. He doesn't deserve to represent justice."

"I'll worry about that in the future," Leo returned. "Right now I am obligated to respond to this bloody summons."

Margaret looked at Leo in visible shock. I wondered why until I remembered that the word "bloody" is a terrible swear word in England. I thought that one of these days I must find out why. This however was not the day.

"What is the date of the inquest?" Robert asked.

"Tomorrow."

"I'll go with you."

"Thank you, Rob."

"I'll go too," I said.

There was a small silence then Leo said, "You cannot accompany me, Isabel. The inquest will be held in a tavern."

"A tavern filled with every local in the area and they all will be drinking," Robert added. "It is not a place for ladies."

I looked from Leo to Robert then back again to Leo. "I grew up in a circus. What kind of people do you think I associated with? I can assure you I won't be uncomfortable if I am surrounded by the lower classes, even if they are drinking."

The men were silent.

Margaret was the one to answer me. "Your station in life has changed Isabel. You are to marry the Earl of Camden, and his countess cannot be seen in local taverns. It would cause a scandal."

I shot back, "If the aristocracy in France had mixed with the lower classes more, they wouldn't have had their heads cut off! The English should learn a lesson from that."

Robert and Margaret stared at me in horror.

Leo said tiredly, "Isabel, sweetheart, this is not the time to discuss French aristocrats. I can assure you that I very frequently mix with the people who work for me. That is not what is at issue here."

Instantly I wanted to kiss away the worry lines on his forehead, but since I couldn't do that I said instead, "All right. I will remain at home. But I want to hear about everything that happens."

"I promise that you will," Leo said.

"Don't worry, Isabel," Robert said seriously. "No one is going to arrest Leo."

"They had better not," I said.

We finished breakfast and the two men departed, leaving me alone with Margaret. She said, "There is something we need to discuss, Isabel."

I looked at her in surprise. Margaret was always pleasant, but we rarely had a private conversation. She said, "When you marry Leo you will become the mistress of this house. You and I must sit down sometime soon so I can show you my books and explain how they are kept."

I looked at her in confusion. "What do you mean?"

"I mean that I have been doing the work of the mistress of the house for years but once you are married it will be your responsibility."

I let these words settle into my mind. I had lived at Camden Hall long enough to understand that the status of each resident was vitally important to them. Margaret was already eclipsed by Aunt Augusta. Now I would be taking away the status she did have. She was not in a comfortable situation.

As I looked at Margaret's strained face an idea struck me like a force of lightning; if something should happen to Leo,

Robert would be the next earl! I absolved Robert of wanting to do away with Leo but what about Robert's wife? Margaret would be a countess if Leo died, and her son would be the future earl.

The more I thought about this idea the more likely it became. If Leo didn't marry again, Robert or his eldest son David would become the earl. And no one in the family had expected Leo to marry again. Everyone thought he would never replace his beloved Catherine.

And then I had come along.

At this point in my musings, reality reared its ugly head. My brother had been shot in the head. Whoever fired that shot had to have been an excellent marksman or incredibly lucky. Either way, it couldn't have been Margaret.

She could have hired someone.

I looked across at my future sister-in-law as she sipped her tea. I had absolutely no proof to support this theory. If I confided it to Leo, he would be furious with me for thinking such a thing. He had great respect for Margaret.

I told Margaret I would be happy to sit down with her at her convenience, bade her good morning and went upstairs to confide in Elisabeth, the only person in the house who might take my idea seriously.

*

Leo and Robert did not return home until teatime. I had passed a horrible day. I actually snapped at Papa when he said something perfectly sensible. I apologized profusely and he assured me he forgave me, but I caught him looking at me worriedly and I returned to the house to leave him in peace.

By the time Leo and Robert appeared I had gone from being worried to being scared. Why were they so late? Robert had assured me that the inquest would be over quickly. Had Leo been arrested? Could Wolcott arrest an earl? Would there be a real trial? Could Leo lose his head?

Leo and Robert were smiling broadly when they came into the drawing room when we were having tea. A shout of joy rose from around the room.

Robert raised his voice, "It's over and Wolcott has been removed from office."

The aunts, my mother, Sir John, Susan and Margaret surrounded the two men in the doorway. I remained where I was. I was well acquainted with the signs of men who have had too much to drink, and the two men standing on the threshold of this room had clearly been drinking. They had been drinking in the pub while I had been at home making myself sick with worry. Quite suddenly I was furious.

Robert was talking, telling everyone that when Leo had given his testimony about being held up because of his horse's shoeing problem and Alcott had asked him to provide proof the entire room had erupted in outrage. How dare the squire ask his lordship for proof? Everyone knew what a fine man his lordship was. It was an insult to ask him to produce two blacksmiths when everyone present knew he would never lie under oath. Not his lordship. Never his lordship. The men who had been called as a jury declared his lordship innocent and joined the crowd. Leo bought drinks for everyone and he and Robert joined the celebration.

He had never once thought that I might be worrying myself sick. I came from a country that cut off nobles' heads when they displeased the crowd. I really hadn't thought Leo would lose his head today, but I was worried he might be arrested. I had been picturing him in prison. And he hadn't once thought to send me word that all was well.

I wanted to leave the room, but it would cause too much speculation among the family if I did, so I remained where I was and waited for Leo to come sit beside me. Eventually he did. I said, "Congratulations on not being arrested."

I could feel him staring at my profile. "What's wrong?" he asked.

"Nothing at all. I'm glad you enjoyed yourself drinking all afternoon at the tavern while I worried myself sick about you. You might have sent me word that all was well."

"Isabel." His voice was patient, the voice you use when speaking to a child. "I told you there was no chance of my being arrested. And you yourself said that it's a good thing for a noble to associate with his inferiors."

I stood up. "I feel a headache coming on. I think I shall retire to my bedroom."

He stood as well. "I will escort you."

I glanced up at him and looked away quickly. His mouth was set in a grim line and his eyes were narrowed. I swallowed. "I don't need your escort."

"Nevertheless, you have it." He took my arm in a firm grasp, said something to Aunt Augusta about my not feeling well, and walked me out of the room.

We went up the stairs in silence, and when we reached my room I tried to pull my arm away while saying, "You have done your duty and escorted me safely to my room. I will see you at dinner."

He tightened his hand, opened the door and walked the two of us inside. I called Elisabeth's name but she didn't answer. I remembered that she took tea with Mrs. Adams this time of day. I looked up at Leo, who was standing too close to me, and said, *"Au Revoir."*

He said, *"I told you not to worry,"* bent his head and kissed me. It was a hard kiss, and I tried to pull away, but then it softened and his body bent over mine. I felt the angry resistance in my own body drain away and my arms slid around his neck so that my body was pressed full length against his. I kissed him back, loving the feel of his strength against me, the feel of his hair under my fingers, the smell of his skin....

Two hard hands gripped my shoulders and lifted me away from him. I looked up, shocked by the interruption. His hair was hanging over his forehead and his neck cloth was disarranged. He said, "This is dangerous, sweetheart. I thought your maid would be here."

My heart was hammering and I was breathing fast.

"I'm sorry I didn't send you word," he said. "I didn't realize you would be worrying."

I looked up into the blue eyes I loved so much. "I'm sorry I was cross. You were right to remain and celebrate with the men who were so loyal to you."

We looked at each other. There was a gap of perhaps two feet of carpet between us and we both wanted desperately to cross it. Leo said, "I will see you at dinner."

"Oui," I replied softly and watched as he walked out the door.

Chapter Twenty-Six

The planning for our wedding took place with little contribution from the bride or groom. Aunt Augusta and Mother were consumed with it, and when asked a question my invariable answer was, "Do whatever you think is best." I don't think either woman minded my disinterest. They were enjoying themselves enormously.

Leo and I spent most of our days with Papa planning our stud farm and riding school. Papa had settled quickly into the charming little house Leo had given him and was cooking for himself until Estelle, our housekeeper from France, arrived. Two of the men who had worked with the circus horses in France were coming as well. They were excellent riders and they were bringing Henri, Papa's horse, with them.

One afternoon, when Leo and I were walking back to the house from the stable, I brought up a subject that had been much on my mind: Margaret. "She needs her own home, Leo," I said persuasively. "When she married Rob and came to live at Camden Hall, she assumed the duties that rightfully belong to the mistress of the house. Aunt Augusta might be your official hostess, but Margaret does all the work. Now that we are getting married I will be expected to assume the duties of the mistress. There can't be two mistresses in the same house, Leo, and Margaret will lose her status."

A lock of hair had fallen across his brow and he pushed it back impatiently. "What does Margaret do that's so important? Wouldn't it be easier for you if she just kept doing whatever it is? You are going to be busy with the new riding school."

I said, spacing my words so they would make an impact, "Leo, if Camden Hall is going to be my house then I want to be the woman who runs it. I do not wish to relinquish the reins to somebody else."

There was a long pause. Leo's brows were drawn together. Clearly he was not happy with my proposal. Finally he said, "I have no intention of replacing Rob as my steward."

"I never said that you should. There's no reason why he can't carry on if they live in another house."

"I need to be able to reach him quickly. He knows more about the estate than I do."

I said in my most reasonable voice, "I know how valuable he is to you and I know how much you care for him. I was wondering about that big house you own that stands half a mile down the road. It's part of the estate property but no one lives in it. What do you call it? The Dover House?"

Amusement glinted in his eyes. "The *Dower* House you mean. Many estates have such a house. It's kept for the widowed mother of the owner to live in when her eldest son marries."

"Thus insuring that there would be only one mistress in the house?"

He lifted his eyebrows, conceding the point, but he didn't respond. I said, "It looks very elegant. The kind of house built for a noble or a rich man. It would give Margaret the status in the community she deserves."

Silence.

I went on, "There's no reason why Robert can't keep his office at Camden. The only difference would be that in the evening he'd go home to the Dower House. It's not even a mile away, Leo. If you should need him in the evening you will be able to reach him quickly."

Leo bent his head and pretended to look at the list of mares we had been contemplating. I regarded the back of his golden head and wanted to tell him what I suspected about Margaret, but I held my tongue. He wouldn't believe me. I had no evidence to back up my suspicions.

We walked in silence up the stone steps that led into the back garden. Finally he said, "I'll miss seeing him at dinner."

"I know. I will too."

"I'll miss the boys."

"They're away at school most of the time. And one day you will have boys of your own to play with."

He stopped walking and looked down at me. "You're set on this aren't you?"

"I am. Margaret needs a house of her own, Leo. She's had enough of doing the work while Aunt Augusta usurps the position that should be hers."

He started walking again using the shorter step he adopted when he was walking with me. As we reached the back door he said, "It might be good for Rob to be the master in his own house. He has lived in my shadow all our lives."

I said gently, "Living in separate houses won't break the bond between you and your brother, Leo. Nothing could ever do that."

Our eyes met and he smiled. I felt that smile through my entire body. "You're right. But the Dower House hasn't been lived in for many years. I'll take a look at it. Work will need to be done before they can move in."

I put a hand on his forearm, feeling the hardness of it through the soft wool of his coat. I said, "Don't have any work done. Present the house to Margaret the way it is and give her a budget to make the changes she wants. Let her make it *her* house."

He thought for a moment then nodded slowly. "All right. If that is what you think she would like."

"I know it is."

"Then we can speak to them tonight after dinner. Even if Rob should prefer to remain at Camden he will agree to the plan. He loves Margaret and what makes her happy will make him happy."

"Thank you." I looked up and gave him my best smile. "You are such a good man, Leo."

"If you keep looking at me that way I will not be a good man much longer."

I laughed and let him hold the door for my entry into the house.

*

Sometime during the day Leo asked Robert if he and Margaret would come to the library after dinner. Of course Robert agreed and once dinner was over the four of us met in the great book-enclosed room. Leo asked Robert and Margaret to sit on the old green velvet sofa and he and I sat on two chairs across from them.

Leo had asked me if I wanted to speak first. Since this move was my idea, I felt obligated to say that I would. Once we were all settled, and Robert and Margaret were looking at us with mystified faces, I began. "The Dower House has been empty for years, and Leo and I would be happy for you to have it for your own family," I said.

They still looked bewildered.

"To live there," I clarified. "Margaret has been the unnoticed chatelaine of this house for years while Aunt Augusta, who does nothing, is Leo's hostess. I believe that Margaret deserves to be the chatelaine of her own house. Especially since Leo is getting married."

Margaret had grown very pale and Robert had grown very red. He said to Leo, "Are you trying to push us out of the house?"

Leo leaned forward in his chair. "Of course not, Rob! I love having you and Margaret and the boys under my roof. But Isabel seems to think that Margaret deserves to have a house of her own."

Robert said, "That's nonsense. We love living here."

Margaret said, "You would really give us the Dower House to live in?"

Leo said, "More than that—I will give you the deed to the Dower House. I think it's time Rob owned some property."

Robert's mouth opened in astonishment.

Margaret said incredulously, "You will make it over to us?"

"I will."

He hadn't told me about this decision and my heart swelled with pride and love.

"But...you might need the Dower House someday," Rob said.

"Rob, it's been standing empty for years. I can't remember the last time it was used. Grandmother lived here at Camden when she was still alive; she didn't move to the Dower House. Remember?"

"That's true," Robert said slowly.

I said, "If I outlive Leo, I will never live in the Dower House. I am more than happy for you to own it."

"There's no reason to keep it standing empty the way it has," Leo said. "It's better that somebody lives there than letting it stand the way it has." He turned his gaze to Margaret who was just beginning to regain her color. "Is Isabel right, Margaret, or do you wish to keep living here in Camden Hall?"

"I would like to live in the Dower House very much," she said in an unsteady voice.

Rob's brows drew together in the exact same way Leo's did when he was puzzled. "Are you sure, Margaret? You never said a word to me about having our own house."

"It's as Isabel said. Once she takes over as mistress of Camden there will be nothing for me to do." Her voice steadied and became firm. She looked directly into Leo's eyes and said, "I would love to have the Dower House for our family."

Robert turned back to Leo. "It's been standing empty for so many years. Is it livable?"

"I took a look at it this afternoon. It's livable but it needs work to turn it into a comfortable home." He smiled at Margaret. "I was planning to hire someone to refurbish it, but Isabel thought you would like to do that yourself. I suggest we get together and go over the house to see what needs to be done. You will definitely have to replace some of the furniture. Once I have an idea of how much money it will cost to bring it up to standard I'll give you a budget and you can send the bills to me."

"No, Leo." Robert's voice was loud and distinct. "I cannot allow you to spend money on a house that won't even be yours. And you need me to be close by. It will be better if we remain here at Camden. Isabel and Margaret will find a way to work together."

Margaret made a small, protesting sound.

Leo said, "You will be half a mile away. You can easily continue as my steward from so great a distance." He leaned forward again and when he spoke his voice was deep and intense. "You are the best brother in the world, Rob. I rely on you all the time and you always know what to do. I want you to have this property to pass down to your children. I'll also increase your salary to accommodate the demands that come with owning property."

"You don't have to do that. You pay me much more than you'd pay a steward who wasn't your brother."

"I was born first, Rob, and I inherited everything. It's the way the world goes but it isn't fair." He looked at Margaret. "Tell him not to argue, Margaret."

"Don't argue with your brother, Robert." The ivory skin of her face flushed. "We will have need of more money since our family will soon be increasing."

Shocked silence. Finally Rob said, "Are you saying that...are you...?" His voice ran out. Margaret smiled radiantly. "Yes, I am saying that we will have another child."

Well, you can imagine. Robert folded Margaret in a tender embrace. Leo and I grinned like idiots. When Robert finally let Margaret go, Leo shook his hand and said, "I am assuming your argument is finished."

Robert was grinning even more than we were. "She can have whatever she likes. We'll take your house, we'll take your money, and in return we'll give you a new niece or nephew."

Leo hugged him then went to kiss Margaret, who was crying. I also hugged Robert and kissed Margaret. Henry's killer had not yet been found and I was extremely glad she would be leaving my house.

Chapter Twenty-Seven

The wedding plans were marching along. Mother and Aunt Jane dragged me into London for an interminable week so I could find the perfect wedding dress. Custom said it had to be white with silver trim. I also had to wear a long lace scarf that was supposed to hang from my head all the way down to my ankles.

Once I was in London, I discovered that picking out the wedding dress was just the start of our shopping. Mother and Aunt Jane had planned to replace all of the dresses I owned with clothing "suitable" to the Countess of Camden. They bought me morning dresses, afternoon dresses, carriage dresses, evening dresses, pelisses, hats, gloves, muffs, stockings, reticules and hair ornaments. When I protested, Aunt Jane laughed and said they didn't trust me ever to buy clothes for myself, and they were going to make certain I was provided for.

Not for the first time I wished that Leo wasn't an earl. It was a fleeting wish, though, and I didn't mean it. Leo *was* an earl. It was in his bones and in his blood. It had formed him from childhood. To wish he wasn't an earl would be to wish he wasn't Leo. It was going to be difficult for me to be a countess, but I was determined to do my best to live up to Leo's standard. So I allowed Mother and Aunt Jane to pick out my clothes. They knew what I needed.

I also knew how important this wedding was to my mother. She had missed seeing me grow up and she was glowing with happiness that she was here for my wedding. I understood this and I did my best to be cooperative. I was unbelievably patient with the long discussions between Mother and Aunt Jane over what dress looked best, what shoes looked best, what hat looked best. When they asked for my opinion I invariably went with my mother's choice.

Sometimes, as I stood in the dress shop modeling a dress, Mother and Aunt Jane circling me with frowns on their faces, I would think of the girl who had arrived at Camden Hall four months ago. I remembered how I had fought becoming a part of the decadent aristocratic family I had been thrust into. They had been as alien as if they lived on another planet. When I looked back on that prickly unhappy girl I realized how much I had changed.

Susan had come with us to London. She was to be my bridesmaid and of course she had to have a special dress too. I sat with saintly patience while she tried on dress after dress in shop after shop and I gave my opinion when I was asked. As the prices for this shopping expedition mounted higher and higher, I wondered who was paying for all this extravagance. When the last of our purchases had been delivered to our hotel I asked Mother that question.

"Susan's father is paying for her dress and Leo is paying for everything else," she replied. "My husband told me he was happy to pay for your wedding dress, but when I mentioned this to Leo he wouldn't hear of it. He was perfectly prepared to pay for the entire wedding, including your bride clothes, and there was to be no more discussion on the subject."

I said, "It was very kind of Sir John to offer to pay for my dress. He is not my father and I only just met him."

"He wanted to pay for it, Isabel," Mother said earnestly. "He is very fond of you."

I put an arm around her shoulder and hugged her. "Tell him I appreciate his offer." I knew he had made the offer for

Mother's sake not for mine, and it was nice to know he cared about her so much.

Finally all of the purchases were delivered and packed into our coach. We had taken Leo's old coach because it afforded more space for storing baggage than did his newer coach. As we drove out of London I leaned back against the cushioned seat and smiled. We were going home.

Home. When I came to Camden Hall I never dreamed I would ever think of it as home. *Home isn't a place, home is people,* I thought. *Wherever Leo and Papa are, that is home for me.*

Then I thought of Alonzo, and amended my previous conclusion. Home is people and a horse.

*

The day of our wedding arrived, and the sun was out. The wedding was scheduled for ten o'clock at St. Michael Church in the village. Camden Hall had its own chapel, but it had not been used for religious purposes for many years. Leo said he preferred the church where he worshipped every Sunday, and so we were to be married at St. Michael.

Mother and I and Elisabeth breakfasted in my room so Leo wouldn't see me before the wedding. After breakfast Mother and Elisabeth helped me dress. After Elisabeth had pinned the circlet of roses that was the headpiece that anchored my lace scarf, I went to look in the mirror. Behind me I heard Mother sniffle. I turned around to see tears streaming down her face.

"Mother!" I went to stand close to her. I didn't dare hug her while I was wearing this hugely expensive dress, but I patted her back. "Is anything wrong?"

"No." She looked at me through her tears. "You just look so beautiful and I am so fortunate to have you back."

Damn the bloody dress, I thought, hugged her and said, "I'm lucky to have found you. I never told you this, but I didn't want to meet you. I thought it would be a betrayal of my mother in heaven if I met you. But now I understand that my mother in heaven wants me to be happy. That's what she wanted when she was on this earth, and I know that's what she wants now. She is glad I have you."

"Thank you, my darling. You are such a generous girl."

I had never thought of myself as generous, but I allowed the comment to pass. My eyes went to Elisabeth. She was crying too. I went to give her a hug and said, "You look beautiful in your new dress. Don't get it wet by crying on it."

She wiped her cheeks with her hand. "I am so h-happy," she said in a strangled voice.

Leo had driven Elisabeth and me into Lambourn to purchase her a dress for the wedding. She was going to sit with Papa at the front of the church. As Elisabeth disappeared into her room to get a handkerchief, a knock came at the door and Susan came in. She looked lovely in the pale blue dress that matched her eyes.

"Ohhh Isabel," she said in a hushed voice. "You look so beautiful."

I looked back in the mirror and saw a tall slender girl in a long white and silver gown. The front of the gown had a small scoop baring my neck (Leo had once called my neck "swanlike") and I wore a single strand of pearls that had belonged to my *Maman*. I didn't know if they were real and I didn't care. They were one of the few ornaments she had owned, and I treasured them. I wore pearl earrings as well, given to me by Aunt Augusta! She told me her father had given them to her when she made her come-out and she wanted me to have them. I had been sincerely touched by her gesture.

When Elisabeth and Mother had repaired their faces, Susan opened the door and held it for the three of us to go out. When we reached the staircase, Susan bent to hold the small train of my dress. "We don't want the bride to fall down the stairs and miss her wedding," she said brightly.

I walked carefully down the grand staircase, which had become as familiar to me as our farmhouse in France. *I'm getting married*, I thought. *Pray for me, Maman. I am getting married!*

Chapter Twenty-Eight

Papa and I rode in Leo's curricle to the church. The hood on the carriage had been put down so that Papa and I would be visible to the people who were lining the streets. "There will be people waiting to see you," Aunt Augusta had warned me, and she was right. The roadway was packed with men, women and children all shouting: *God bless you, my lady! Isn't she beautiful? Look at her veil—it's made all of lace!*

Papa and I were accustomed to performing in front of large crowds and we knew what to do. We smiled and waved at the kind people who had probably been standing for hours waiting for the carriage to arrive.

At last we reached St Michael, a gray stone church with a tall stone tower. A graveyard lay to its left and evenly cut grass grew on a small lawn in front. I had been to church with Leo and Aunt Augusta every Sunday since I arrived at Camden Hall and both the church and the vicar were familiar to me.

Susan was waiting for us on the steps and after Papa had helped me to alight, she picked up my train so it wouldn't get dirty. We ascended the stairs and entered into the vestibule. Papa went down the aisle to join Mother and Elisabeth in the front row and I peered through the glass that divided the vestibule from the main body of the church, hoping to see Leo.

All of the local gentry had come out; every pew was taken. I could see Leo standing at the top of the aisle with his groomsman, Robert of course, standing beside him. I stepped away from the window, steadier now that I had seen him.

Susan was commenting on the filled church and I said, "They've all come for Leo. I think everyone is happy to see him getting married again."

Everyone but Margaret, I thought to myself. Leo and I were taking a few weeks' honeymoon at a property he owned in Hampshire. By the time we returned my hope was that Margaret and Robert would be moved into the Dower House. She might be perfectly innocent of wishing ill to Leo. She probably was perfectly innocent. But no one else had been caught and I would feel better with her out of his way.

Susan said, "When you first came to Camden did you ever think you would marry Leo?"

"Never. I hated him for making me leave my Papa. I hated everything about Camden, and I was desperately lonely. All I wanted to do was hide in Alonzo's stall for the next six months. Leo understood how unhappy I was, and he took me riding with him. That's when I got to know him."

Susan sighed. "It's so romantic. I hope I can find a husband to love the way you love Leo."

I didn't think she would. I didn't think anyone could love a man as much as I loved Leo. But I smiled and said, "I'm sure you will one day."

The organ began to play, and I inhaled deeply. Susan said, "It's time."

I nodded. We both moved to the door that opened onto the center aisle of the church and began to process slowly, me first and Susan behind watching over my train. After the first few careful steps I looked down the aisle and saw Leo. He was wearing a light gray morning coat and pale gray pantaloons. The sun shone through the stained-glass windows that surrounded the altar and lit his hair. I was too far away to see the expression on his face.

Everyone was standing and singing the opening hymn. It wasn't one I had heard before and I thought it must be a wedding hymn. I came abreast of my mother and saw there were tears rolling down her cheeks. I paused, leaned over the pew end, and kissed her. She smiled through her tears and I went forward again.

The wedding ceremony was lovely. Papa said he would give me to Leo. I promised to take Leo as my wedded husband. I promised to have him for better for worse, for richer for poorer, in sickness and health, to love, cherish, and obey until death. I didn't mind promising to obey Leo. I couldn't imagine him ever asking me to do something I didn't want to do. And if he did…well we would discuss it. Leo put a delicate gold ring on my finger, and we were pronounced Man and Wife.

We looked into each other's eyes as those words were said and I felt…I felt….how to describe it? How my heart was so full of love it swelled in my chest until I could hardly breathe, how my body was quivering and my hand trembling, how I just wanted to fling my arms around Leo and hold him tight. He bent his head and kissed me. "It's legal now," he said and grinned.

The grin was what restored my composure. I smiled back at him. Susan fussed with my train and together we walked back down the aisle as husband and wife.

*

Leo and I drove back to the house in the curricle. A huge wedding breakfast had been set out in the dining room for all of the guests. Tents had been set up on the front lawn for the servants' and tenants' festivities. A crowd of adults and children was already spread across the thick green grass, many of them already eating the food that was being served in the tents.

Everyone cheered as our curricle rolled by, and Leo and I waved at the excited children. We were only staying for part of the wedding breakfast; then we would change our clothes and leave for Waltham House in Hampshire. Leo had sent a contingent of servants down two days before to make sure the house was ready for us. Elisabeth and Leo's valet were leaving as soon as they changed out of their wedding clothes so they would be at Waltham to greet us. They were traveling in the carriage with all of our baggage.

This swarm of servants was Leo's idea of a private, quiet honeymoon. I may have rolled my eyes a few times as he made his preparations, but I didn't say a word.

I did speak my mind one time though. It was a week before the wedding, and Leo and I had taken the horses for a morning ride. We had stopped at the river, dismounted and gone to stand beside the clear rushing water. I was leaning against his shoulder not thinking about anything except how lovely it was to be here with him, when he said, "I haven't given you a wedding gift yet. Is there something special you would like?"

"Leo, two nights ago you presented me with a fortune in jewelry. That is a huge wedding present."

A breeze kicked up and ruffled my hair. He smoothed a stray lock behind my ear. His touch made me shiver.

"That jewelry belongs to the estate, sweetheart. It's on loan to you for as long as you are the earl's wife. I want to give you something that will be yours to keep."

I rubbed my cheek against his shoulder. "I will have you to keep."

"Thank you, darling, but I meant something other than me."

I wondered if this was the time to bring up something I had been considering recently. I rubbed my cheek against his shoulder once more and said calmly, "I would like a new cook for a wedding present."

I felt him stiffen. "A new cook? What is wrong with the cook we have?"

I knew that if I didn't speak now I never would. I summoned my courage and said, "Leo, I am sorry to have to say this, but I think we should always be honest with each other. The food at Camden Hall is atrocious."

His brows went up. His eyes enlarged. "Atrocious? I know it's plain English cooking, Isabel, but I certainly wouldn't call it *atrocious*."

I hated hurting his feelings and was tempted to give in. Then I remembered that I was going to have to eat that cooking or cooking like it for the rest of my life. I steeled my heart and said, "You asked me what I wanted for a wedding present and that is my answer. "I want a French chef."

"A French chef!"

"Leo, you live in London for part of the year. There must be houses in London that have French chefs. Have you never eaten French cooking?"

Long pause, then he said reluctantly, "The Jerseys have a French chef."

"Have you eaten there?"

"Yes."

"Was it good?"

His nostrils quivered. "Yes."

"Better than 'plain English cooking'?"

He threw up his hands. "Isabel, what am I supposed to do with Mrs. Sarett? She's been cooking for us for years! She came to Camden when my father was still the earl!"

"Retire her," I said. "Find her a nice house and give her a pension."

"I never thought you could be so heartless." The poor man looked truly shocked.

"Leo, why do you think Papa moved into his new house before Estelle arrived? He'd rather cook for himself than eat what appears on our table. I can cook better than Mrs. Sarett."

"She's been here forever," he said stubbornly.

"Talk to her. You might be surprised. She might be happy to retire. How old is she?"

"I don't know."

"If she's been here since your father's time, she can't be young. Talk to her," I repeated.

And that was how we left it.

*

The wedding "breakfast" was really a luncheon, but there were some breakfast foods on the table as well. Leo helped himself to sausage and blood pudding and I chose a plate of cold turkey. Then we moved into the drawing room where the guests—all of them suitably high born—had gathered with their food. Champagne was being poured and I accepted a glass. Aunt Augusta was seated before the fireplace and she beckoned me to her side. I made my way to her, balancing the food and the glass as I wove through the crowd. For the next hour I was introduced to a collection of earls, viscounts, barons and their wives. Everyone told me I looked beautiful and said how wonderful it was that Leo was marrying again.

While I stood trapped next to Aunt Augusta, Leo had been circling the room chatting to as many people as possible. After an hour and a half he finally arrived at my side. I prayed he was going to rescue me, and he did.

"Isabel and I are going upstairs to change our clothes now, Aunt Augusta," he said. "We need to leave soon if we are to reach Hampshire in time for dinner."

"Very well, dear boy." She looked at the both of us and I thought I saw the glisten of tears in her eyes. "I am so happy for you both. Isabel, my dear," her veined old hand pulled me toward her. "God bless you," she said. I bent down and kissed her cheek. "Thank you, Aunt Augusta. You have been so kind to me."

"Oh dear child." Those definitely were tears in her eyes. "You have been such a gift to us. To see Leo marry again...it's made my heart burst with joy."

I stepped back and let Leo take my place. He too bent and kissed the old lady on her cheek. He straightened up and grinned at her. "I am a happy man today, Aunt."

"Indeed you are. You are a good man, Leo. You have put up with your old aunt for all these years, and never once have you made me feel I am unwelcome in your home." Two tears actually rolled down her cheeks. "God bless you, my boy. God bless you both."

We left her side both of us feeling a little stunned. "Was that actually Aunt Augusta?" I said.

"When my father died she went into full mourning. She loves us all very much, but she doesn't know how to show it."

I made a resolution never to say another unkind word about Aunt Augusta no matter the provocation.

An hour later Leo and I were in the saddle heading toward Waltham House. Mother had protested when she heard we were riding, but I explained we wanted to have our horses in Hampshire, and we didn't trust anyone else to get them there safely. Leo assured her that the trip would be less than three hours.

Elisabeth was already on her way to Hampshire, so Mother helped me out of my wedding gown. When I was standing in my chemise and petticoat she said, "Darling, do you know what happens on a wedding night? I knew nothing about it when I married Mansfield and the shock was awful."

I kissed her cheek. "I grew up in a circus, Mother. I know all about what goes on between a male and female when they mate."

"I see. Have you ever…?" Her voice trailed off.

"No, Mother, I have never."

"Thank God. What would Leo say if he found you were not a virgin?"

"I expect he would continue to love me just the same."

The worried lines disappeared from her forehead and she gave me a lovely smile. "I'm sure he would. One has only to look at the two of you together to know there is something special between you."

When I was dressed in my riding clothes and my wedding dress was hanging off the door of my wardrobe, I gave Mother a kiss and went downstairs to meet my husband.

Chapter Twenty-Nine

Waltham House was a pretty gabled manor house surrounded by lawns, meadows and woods. Leo told me it had been built during the reign of Queen Anne and had come into his family through the business dealings of a previous earl. It was a small property, which was why Leo had chosen it for our honeymoon.

We dismounted and two grooms from Camden came down the path to take our reins. "Are the stables decent?" I asked Danny, the groom who was holding Alonzo.

"A little old but we fixed up two grand stalls for Alonzo and Walter," he answered in his Irish accent. "Your boy will be fine, my lady."

Alonzo knew Danny so I felt comfortable he would be well taken care of. As the horses were led away we turned toward the house. Two people were waiting in front of the open door, Denver, the under butler from Camden, and a plump elderly woman with rosy cheeks. She curtseyed deeply when we reached her and introduced herself as Mrs. Wilson, the housekeeper.

The house was as pretty inside as it was outside. The front hall had beams in the roof, mellow oak paneling on the walls and a lovely carved oak staircase. We followed Mrs. Wilson up to the second floor and along a narrow hallway until she opened a door at the very end.

"This will be your bedroom," she said, and we followed her inside. The wood paneling in this room had been painted a rich cream and the wide planked floor was partially covered by a blue and cream rug. An embroidered spread covered the bed and a chaise longue stood in front of the fireplace. The room faced west and the sun from four tall windows was streaming in.

I crossed to the window and looked out at the grounds. I heard Leo say, "Thank you, Mrs. Wilson. This is very nice indeed. If you will have some hot water sent up, we will be ready for dinner at seven."

The housekeeper assured Leo that dinner would be ready at the stipulated time and left. An odd feeling of strangeness had been creeping over me ever since we entered the bedroom. I turned from the window and said, "Where are Elisabeth and Gregory?"

"Probably awaiting us in our dressing rooms." He nodded toward a door on the right wall. "I believe that is yours, sweetheart."

"Oh." I looked on the opposite wall and saw another door. "And that is yours?"

"It is. I suggest we both wash up, change our clothes and go down to dinner."

I was anxious to see Elisabeth and went readily to the door Leo had pointed out. She was inside, sitting on a chintz-covered chair and working on her embroidery. She put it aside as I walked in, and I ran to give her a hug. I was very glad that she was with me. I loved my newly found mother, but it was Elisabeth who had been there for me after *Maman* died. It was Elisabeth who really knew me.

I hugged her harder than usual and she held me close. "A little nervous?" she whispered in my ear.

I sat in her lap. "A little," I said in a small voice. "My life is going to change a lot, isn't it?"

"It is. You will not have the freedom you were accustomed to, *mon ange*. You will always have to take into account how your actions will reflect upon his lordship."

"I know." I had known that when I accepted Leo's proposal. But I was realizing belatedly that I was not the only person who would be affected. When we were traveling with the circus Elisabeth and I had often shared a bed. At Camden Hall she had been in the room next to mine. Where would she sleep now? What position would she have in an earl's household?

Elisabeth was my family as surely as Papa was my family.

She came with me to Camden because I needed her, and she had occupied an awkward position in that aristocratic household. It hadn't mattered so much when I thought I would be staying only six months. Now Camden would be my permanent home. Where would Elisabeth fit in?

I said in a rush, "I have been so selfish, Lisa. I never once thought about how my marriage would affect you. Do you hate being at Camden Hall? You're not part of the family and you're not a servant. I have been thinking about myself so much that I have ignored your position. I am so sorry!"

To my horror I started to cry.

"Stop this right now." It was Elisabeth's stern voice. "I like Camden Hall. I like Mrs. Adams and I like Hobbs. I don't like the food, but I can always eat with M. Pierre and Estelle when she arrives. His lordship told me he was creating a suite of rooms for me in the old part of the house, close to your sitting room. I am to have my own bedroom, sitting room and a small dining room should I like to have guests."

I lifted my head from her shoulder. "He never said a word to me."

"He told me it should be ready by the time we get back home." She smoothed my hair back off my forehead. "He wanted it to be a surprise."

Two things struck me. The first was that Leo had thought of Elisabeth and I hadn't. The second was that she had referred to Camden Hall as *home.*

"Leo is such a good man," I said in a wavering voice.

"He loves you, Isabel. He will always put you first. And you must do the same for him."

"I will," I promised her.

"Do you think you are ready to change your clothes now?"

I wiped the tears from my eyes and smiled at her. "Yes. I am ready."

A knock came upon the door that led into the passageway. I removed myself from Elisabeth's lap and went to the door. One of the footmen from Camden was outside holding a pitcher of water.

"Hello Willie," I said. "How are they treating you here?"

"Very well, my lady. There's only a small staff. No one lives here anymore."

"I'm sorry you had to miss the party at Camden."

"That's all right, my lady. His lordship gave us something extra for coming."

Naturally Leo would think of the staff.

Elisabeth poured the hot water into the bowl and I washed up. Then she helped me into one of the new gowns she had so carefully packed. I would always think it ridiculous to get so formally dressed just to eat dinner, but this was how Leo's people did things and I would conform. "I will see you later, Lisa," I said as I prepared to go down to dinner.

She smiled.

We ate dinner in a lovely room. All of the leaves had been taken out of the table and Henry, another one of our footmen, waited on us. The food was quite decent.

"Who is the cook here, Henry?" I asked.

"Mr. and Mrs. Wilson do the cooking, my lady," he answered. "They be the ones cooking for us these last days."

I looked at my new husband. "What do you think of the food, Leo?" I asked innocently.

He gave me a wary look. "It's good."

"Do you notice that the roast has pink in the middle? That's why it's so tender. It hasn't been overcooked."

He took another bite of roast and didn't answer me. I decided my wedding night was probably not the best time to advocate for a French chef.

After dinner we took a walk to the stable so I could check on Alonzo. He was eating his hay, but when I called his name he came to the front of his stall. I gave him some sugar and rubbed along his neck under his mane, the way he liked. My little session with Elisabeth and now seeing Alonzo made me feel more like myself, and when Leo came to stand behind me I turned my head and smiled at him.

Chapter Thirty

As we walked along the path leading to the house I said wistfully, "This is such a nice little house. Too bad we can't live here all year round."

I could hear the smile in Leo's voice. "There isn't enough room here for a stud and a riding school."

He was right. What had I been thinking? Camden Hall was the perfect location for what Leo had planned. Suddenly I thought of something I hadn't told him yet. "Papa told me he might be able to get one of the horses from Saumur who is due for retirement. A horse like that would be perfect for the school."

We talked enthusiastically about the prospect of getting a Saumur horse, and by the time we reached the house I was actually looking forward to getting back to Camden. We entered the house by the side door and went up to our respective dressing rooms. Elisabeth was sitting in the same chair working on the same embroidery piece when I came in. "Did you eat dinner?" I asked.

She put down her embroidery. "I ate in the kitchen with Mr. and Mrs. Wilson and the rest of the staff. The food was quite good."

"I know." I lowered my voice. "I am trying to get Leo to retire Mrs. Sarett and hire a French chef."

Elisabeth lowered her voice too. "That would be wonderful, Isabel. I have a cousin who is an excellent chef. He would be thrilled to work in the house of an English noble and he would be much cheaper than any of these puffed-up 'geniuses' who make far more money than they're worth."

"I'll tell Leo."

She laughed. "Not tonight, *mon ange.* Please do not talk about cooks tonight."

I smiled and let her unbutton the back of my dress. When she had me out of my dinner dress and into my very flimsy nightdress, I walked to the door that led from the dressing room into the bedroom and put my ear against the wood. "I don't think Leo is there yet."

"I think he will probably wait for you to be in bed before he comes." Elisabeth had been married once when she was very young, so she knew about these things.

"Oh." I felt a strange reluctance to enter that room. It wasn't that I didn't love and trust Leo. It was that I was completely naked under a gown that clearly showed my body and I was...embarrassed.

Elisabeth kissed my cheek and opened the door. A maid had turned down the covers and plumped up the pillows. "Isn't that bed rather small for the both of us?" I asked Elisabeth. "Leo is a big man."

"I'm sure you'll fit." She gave me a little push and I realized I was being a baby about this wedding night. I wasn't afraid. It was just that my body had belonged to just me for all my life. I tried to conjure up how I felt when Leo kissed me, but I had had my clothes on then.

"Get into the bed, Isabel." Elisabeth's voice was soft but definite.

I walked to the side of the bed, which was so high there was a step stool next to it. I stepped on the stool and sat on the bed. I sat up against the pillow and arranged my nightdress so that the folds covered me. Then I pulled the covers up to my waist. Elisabeth had left my hair loose and it tumbled down past my shoulders. She said, "You look lovely, *mon ange*. Don't worry. His Lordship will take care of you."

She closed the dressing room door and I schooled my thoughts. There was no doubt in my mind that I loved Leo. He was a wonderful man. I liked it when he touched my shoulder, or my arm. I liked holding hands with him. I liked kissing him very much.

On this last thought the other dressing room door opened and Leo came into the room. He was holding a candlestick and he put it down on the table next to the bed. He wore a black brocade dressing gown and he sat next to me on my side of the bed. He didn't have to use the step stool.

His blue eyes looked directly into mine, and what he saw caused a line to appear between his eyebrows. "Are you nervous, sweetheart?" he asked.

His voice was so gentle. He looked so concerned. I loved him so much. "Just a little. I've never done this before you see."

He reached out and gathered me close to him, so close that I could feel the beating of his heart. I looked up and said. "I love you, Leo." I repeated Elisabeth's words, "And I trust you to take care of me."

"I will always take care of you, my love. I will spend the rest of my life taking care of you."

The candle on the side table picked out the cleanly chiseled bones of his cheeks, nose and jaw. He bent his head and kissed me. It was a kiss that started tenderly but deepened when I responded. He laid me back against the pillow, still kissing me. I buried my hand in the thickness of his golden hair and everything in me answered to that kiss. His hand moved to cover my breast and I was shocked by the spasm of pleasure that shot through me.

He kissed my ear, my temple, my cheek and then his mouth moved down to my breast. I felt the touch of his lips all the way down in my stomach. He slid the strap of my nightdress down my shoulder and said, "Perhaps we could discard this very pretty nightdress."

I helped him take it off me with no thought of embarrassment. He stood to remove his dressing gown and I stared in wonderment at his broad chest and shoulders, his narrow waist and hips, his long, muscled legs. He was so beautiful. When he came back to me I raised my arms to receive him. I ran my hands up and down his bare arms and felt the strength and power of him under my fingers. I said his name and he kissed me again. After a moment my tongue began to follow the rhythm of his until I was so dizzy I couldn't think. I was drowning in sensation. I felt my hips arch up toward him and he moved until he was poised over me.

He looked down at me and in the candlelight his eyes looked almost black. "This might hurt, sweetheart," he said in a husky voice. "The first time usually hurts."

"I don't care," I said.

He groaned and moved and then he was in me. And he was right—it did hurt. And I was right—I didn't care. I gave my body to him because I loved him, and when he was done, and I held his sweaty body close to me and felt the hammering of his heart and the heaving of his breath, all I felt was happiness that I had been able to give this to him.

We fell asleep in each other's arms, and Elisabeth had been right again, the bed was big enough for both of us. When I woke in the morning Leo was lying next to me, propped up on his elbows, his chin on his clasped hands, his eyes on my face. When I saw him there I smiled.

"I'm sorry I hurt you, sweetheart," he said. "Are you all right?"

His hair was hanging over his forehead and his beautiful blue eyes were full of concern. Oh, how I loved this man. I gave him a smile I knew must be radiant. "I am so happy that now I am really your wife," I said.

He reached out and drew me close. "Thank you, Isabel." His voice was grave. "Thank you for loving me."

I understood what he meant, and I said, "I will always love you, Leo. And I will always stand by you."

He kissed the top of my head. "I believe you. That is the miracle. I believe you."

We lay together in peace until my stomach growled.

"Are you hungry, my love?" he asked in amusement.

"Starving. How about you?"

"Starving. I suggest we go down to breakfast."

"First we have to put on some clothes."

"True. But that means I have to let go of you."

"It does."

He sighed loudly. "Very well." He sat up and swung his legs over the side of the bed presenting me with an impressive view of well-muscled shoulders and back. He picked up his discarded dressing gown and I watched as he walked to his dressing room door. I got out of bed myself and put on my discarded nightdress. Elisabeth would be waiting to help me change and I suspected she would know from one look at my face that Leo had taken very good care of me indeed.

Epilogue

It was warm and sunny the day my son was christened; a perfect September day for his first journey. He was not going very far, only to St. Michael Church to be baptized. I had been there for a baptism only a few months before when Robert and Margaret's baby girl had been christened. They had asked me to be godmother and I had been deeply touched.

They were living now in the Dower House and Margaret and I had become good friends. My attitude toward my sister-in-law had changed dramatically when we found out who was the real murderer of my brother. This occurred as soon as we returned from our honeymoon. One of Leo's tenants told him in confidence that John Brace, another tenant of Leo's, had shot Henry because he had raped Brace's thirteen-year-old daughter Ellen. When she had come home crying hysterically and the bloodstains had sustained her story, Brace had gone berserk.

A few of Brace's good friends knew what had happened. They hadn't spoken up because they knew Leo would never be charged and they had sympathy for Brace. "They probably would have done the same thing themselves," Leo had said when he told me.

So Henry's murder went unsolved and I felt terrible that I had suspected Margaret. We became quite close when she found out I was expecting a child as well. She and Elisabeth had been with me during the birth. My mother had come to Camden as well and arrived in time to hold a squalling infant in her arms.

Leo wanted to call the baby Peter after my Papa, and I cried when he told me that. I cried quite a lot while I was pregnant. But I rode into my seventh month (to the loud disapproval of Aunt Augusta) and Alonzo carried me as carefully as if I were a basket of eggs.

I stood on the front steps with Elisabeth as the christening party set off for the church. Margaret was holding Peter in her arms as Robert carefully guided the two of them into the carriage Leo had presented them with as a gift for their new home. They were to be Peter's godparents. Sir John and Mother went in their carriage; Susan, Aunt Jane and Sir Alexander Repton went in their carriage; and Leo went with Papa and Aunt Augusta in our carriage. It was only two weeks after Peter's birth, and I had not been churched yet, so I remained at home.

Elisabeth remained with me. She adored Peter but I was still first with her. It was probably selfish of me, but I was happy I was still first in her heart.

"You should rest until the christening party returns," she said as Hobbs closed the front door behind us. "I will check in the kitchen to make certain that everything is in order."

I was feeling tired. I, who could ride forever and still feel energetic, was feeling tired at nine o'clock in the morning. I sighed and said, "Thank you, Lisa."

She put an arm around my shoulders and squeezed. "It's natural to be tired after childbirth, *mon ange*. And the *bebe* took a long time before he decided to be born."

He certainly had, I thought. I had first felt pains during dinner and Peter hadn't been born until eleven the following morning. Robert told me that Leo had paced ceaselessly for the entire time I was in labor. Even Papa, who was nervous himself, had tried to calm Leo down. After the baby had been born, and Elisabeth finally let Leo into the room, I had taken one look at his face and thought he looked worse than I must.

The riding school and accompanying stable had been built and Saumur had sent three mares to be bred to Alonzo. I had been afraid that being a stud might interfere with Alonzo's interest in equitation, but he was his old wonderful self whenever I got into the saddle.

Papa was happy. Elisabeth and I had dinner with him and Estelle at his house once or twice a week, and of course we worked together with the horses. Gypsy was doing remarkably well, especially for a thoroughbred. We had three enthusiastic young men whom Papa was teaching to ride properly. Magnus, our Saumur retiree, had proved to be perfect for a beginner.

And we had a French chef! When Leo asked Mrs. Sarett about retiring, she had been thrilled. It seems her sister had a cottage near the coast in Hampshire and if Mrs Sarett had a pension she could go to live with her. So Leo hired Elisabeth's cousin, who was a marvelous cook. Even Leo admitted the food was much better.

Aunt Augusta was still with us, but I knew she loved us and that thought made her "advice" easier to tolerate. She watched me like a hawk the whole time I was pregnant and was ecstatic that Leo now had an heir.

The christening party returned, and the luncheon went well. Everyone would be staying for at least one night so the house was full. I loved my new family. It was wonderful to know that Peter would grow up with all of these people to love him.

I went to up to bed early. I was nursing Peter (to Aunt Augusta's horror) and my schedule now revolved around him. He had just finished and was asleep in my arms when Leo opened the door. He crossed the bedroom floor to the chair where I was sitting and knelt beside me.

I smiled up at him. "He's had his dinner and now he's sleeping. He'll wake up in a few hours and want to nurse again. Infants have a very simple life."

He knelt, looked at the child sleeping in my arms and said, "I never told you this, but I was so afraid of your giving birth. I was afraid that God would punish me for wanting Catherine and her child to die by taking you too."

I was astonished. I had never once suspected he might be harboring such a fear. "Robert said you were frantic when I was in labor. Was that the reason?"

He nodded. "I couldn't get it out of my mind." He gave me a crooked smile. "They were the worst hours of my entire life, Isabel."

"Oh darling." I used the same soft voice I used when I spoke to my baby. "God isn't like that."

"I know that. But..." He heaved a deep sigh. "I will thank Him every day for the rest of my life for the gift of my wife and my son."

Of course the tears sprang to my eyes. He bent and kissed them away. Then he kissed the baby's head—so softly, so gently, that more tears fell. He lifted his head and looked at me with brilliantly blue eyes. He said, "When are you going to introduce Peter to Alonzo?"

I laughed through my tears. "How about tomorrow?"

"Tomorrow it is," he said, and slipped his arm along the back of the chair to cradle both the baby and me. I rested my head on his broad shoulder and thanked the good God for giving me this joy.

About the Author

Joan Wolf is a *USA TODAY* bestselling author whose highly reviewed books include some forty novels set in the period of the English Regency. She fell in love with the Regency when she was a young girl and discovered the novels of Georgette Heyer. Although she has strayed from the period now and then, it has always remained her favorite.

Joan was born and brought up in New York City, but has spent most of her adult life with her husband and two children in Connecticut. She has a passion for animals, and over the years has filled the house with a variety of much-loved dogs and cats. Her great love for her horses has spilled over into every book she has written. The total number of her published novels is fifty-three, and she has no plans to retire.

"Joan Wolf never fails to deliver the best."
—Nora Roberts

"Joan Wolf is absolutely wonderful. I've loved her work for years."
—Iris Johansen

"As a writer, she's an absolute treasure."
—Linda Howard

"Strong, compelling fiction."
—Amanda Quick

"Joan Wolf writes with an absolute emotional mastery that goes straight to the heart."
—Mary Jo Putney

"Wolf's Regency historicals are as delicious and addictive as dark, rich, Belgian chocolates."
—Publishers Weekly

"Joan Wolf is back in the Regency saddle—hallelujah!"
—Catherine Coulter

* * *

To sign up for Joan's newsletter, email her at joanemwolf@gmail.com.

CPSIA information can be obtained
at www.ICGtesting.com
Printed in the USA
BVHW030125061020
590379BV00001B/9